WISCONSIN WEREWOLVES

Here's what readers from around the country are saying about Johnathan Rand's *AMERICAN CHILLERS:*

" I read THE MICHIGAN MEGA-MONSTERS in one day!"
Johnathan Rand's books are AWESOME!
-Ray M., age 11, Michigan

"When I read FLORIDA FOG PHANTOMS, it really
creeped me out! What a great story!"
-Carmen T., age 11, Washington, D.C.

"Johnathan Rand's books are my favorite.
They're really creepy and scary!"
-Jeremy J., age 9, Illinois

"My whole class loves your books! I have two
of them and they are really, really cool."
-Katie R., age 12, California

"I never liked to read before, but now I read
all the time! The 'Chillers' series is great!"
-Lauren B., age 10, Ohio

"I love AMERICAN CHILLERS because they
are scary, but not too scary, because I don't want
to have nightmares."
-Adrian P., age 11, Maine

"I loved it when Johnathan Rand came to our
school. He was really funny. His books are great."
-Jennifer W., age 8, Michigan

"Johnathan Rand is my favorite author!"
-Kelly S., age 8, Michigan

"AMERICAN CHILLERS are great. I got one
for Christmas, and I loved it. Now, my sister
is reading it. When she's done, I'm going to
read it again."
-Joel F., age 13, New York

"I like the CHILLERS books because they are
fun to read. They are scary, too."
-Hannah K., age 11, Minnesota

"I read the MEGA-MONSTERS book and I
really liked it. Mr. Rand is a great writer."
-Ryan M., age 12, Arizona

"I LOVE AMERICAN CHILLERS!"
-Zachary R., age 8, Indiana

"I read your book to my little sister and
she got freaked out. I did, too!"
-Jason J., age 12, Ohio

"These books are my favorite! I love reading them!"
-Sarah N., age 10, New Jersey

"Your books are great. Please write more so I can read them.
-Dylan H., age 7, Tennessee

Other books by Johnathan Rand:

AMERICAN CHILLERS

AMERICA'S #1 SERIES FOR MAXIMUM CHILLS!

#7: Wisconsin Werewolves

Johnathan Rand

An AudioCraft Publishing, Inc. book

This book is a work of fiction. Names, places, characters and incidents are used fictitiously, or are products of the author's very active imagination.

Book storage and warehouses provided by Chillermania!©
Indian River, Michigan

Warehouse security provided by:
Lily Munster and Scooby-Boo

American Chillers #7: Wisconsin Werewolves
ISBN 13-digit: 978-1-893699-43-4

Librarians/Media Specialists:
PCIP/MARC records available at www.americanchillers.com

Cover illustration by Dwayne Harris
Cover layout and design by Sue Harring

Dickinson Press Inc. Grand Rapids, MI USA Job # 38935 06/20/2011

Wisconsin
Werewolves

VISIT CHILLERMANIA!

WORLD HEADQUARTERS FOR BOOKS BY JOHNATHAN RAND!

Visit the HOME for books by Johnathan Rand! Featuring books, hats, shirts, bookmarks and other cool stuff not available anywhere else in the world! Plus, watch the American Chillers website for news of special events and signings at *CHILLERMANIA!* with author Johnathan Rand! Located in northern lower Michigan, on I-75! Take exit 313 . . . then south 1 mile! For more info, call (231) 238-0338. And be afraid! Be veeeery afraaaaaaiiiid . . . .

Hide and seek. That's the game we were playing one night. The night that everything started to happen.

It's one of my favorite games to play, especially after dark. I'm great at finding places to hide.

There were six of us playing on this particular night. Sometimes there's as many as twelve, which can be really fun.

But tonight wasn't going to be much fun. Oh, it started out fun . . . but that's not the way it ended up.

"Jeremy!"

My mom's voice echoed down the block and through the small forest where we were playing. We'd been outside for a couple of hours, and the sun had just set. It would be really dark soon, and then it would be a *lot* of fun.

"Jeremy!"

Drats. That was the second time. When Mom calls, I'm supposed to holler back so she knows where I'm at. Problem is, if I yelled now, Colette might find me. She was 'it', and I could hear her searching in the forest not far from where I was hiding.

"Jeremy! Answer me!"

I had no choice. If I didn't answer Mom, she'd come looking for me. Then I'd *really* be in trouble.

"I'm fine Mom!" I shouted out the words as quickly as I could. I hoped that I didn't give away my hiding place to Colette!

"Thirty more minutes!" Mom hollered back from far away. Then I heard our front door close.

Well, I thought, *I'm sure Colette heard me. I just*

12

hope she can't hear me well enough to find out where I am hiding.

And I was hiding in a pretty good spot, I must admit. I found a spruce tree that had branches growing all the way to the ground, and I climbed within the thick, prickly limbs and hunkered to the ground as close as I possibly could. I knew that if I could just stay quiet, Colette would never find me here.

Crunch. Crunch-crunch.

I could hear Colette getting closer and closer. I knew she'd heard me, but I was hidden really well.

Crunch. Ker-snap.

She'd stepped on a branch, and stopped.

This is too cool, I thought. She was only a few feet away, but she would never find me here!

An owl hooted from far off. A mosquito buzzed by my ear. Stars began twinkling in the rapidly-coming night.

Crunch.

Colette took a step, and, for the first time, I could see her silhouette in the shadows. She wasn't far away at all. I just needed to sit tight and not make a sound.

Then I heard a voice from farther away:

"Tag! You're it!"

It was Colette . . . but that was impossible! Colette was standing just a few feet in front of me!

I could hear the crunch and snap of twigs as others emerged from their hiding places — but the figure in front of me didn't move. I must have mistaken someone else for Colette.

I pushed a branch away, and the needles scraped my arm as I stood up.

"I knew she'd never find me," I said to the person standing near. "That's a great hiding spot, there."

Whoever it was, they didn't speak. Instead, I heard a sniffing sound, like a dog that has picked up the scent of something.

"Who are you?" I asked, knowing that it could only be one of four other friends who were playing hide and seek.

No answer.

"Hey, suit yourself," I said, and I began walking away . . . until I heard a low growl.

"Funny," I said, pulling out a small flashlight from my pocket. "Real funny." I clicked on the flashlight, shined it directly into the face of whoever it was . . . and received the shock of my life. The figure before me wasn't one of my friends. It had a hairy face, and a long, sharp nose. Long fangs dripped over the edges of his mouth, and its black eyes glowed an eerie yellow in the gleam of the flashlight.

Right then and there, I knew what it was.

I was face to face — with a werewolf.

I screamed and spun at the same time. I had to get away, and fast.

"Ahhhhhhgggggghhhhh!!!" I cried out as I ran through the brush. Branches whipped at my face and scratched at my arms. Limbs reached out like spiny arms, and I nearly tripped and fell.

"Jeremy!" I heard Colette call out. *"Where are you?!?! What's the matter?!?!"*

"I'm here!" I shouted. "Help me!"

I found the trail that weaves through the woods and ran lickety-split, fast as my legs would carry me, toward our home base. Actually, it's just a small clearing in the woods where we all gather to begin our games of hide and seek.

I ran and ran, not daring to look behind me for fear of seeing the dark figure of the werewolf. I'd heard that werewolves were really fast, and I didn't want to take any chances.

It was growing darker and darker, and I didn't notice the figures coming toward me on the trail until it was too late. I smacked into someone dead-on, and we both went flying, along with two people that were right behind him. I heard Colette gasp as she hit the ground, and then Tyler Norris. Colette and Tyler are two of my best friends.

"Jeremy!" Tyler said as he rolled on the ground. "What's the matter?!?!?"

"Run!" I said, getting to my feet. "There's a werewolf after me!"

"What?!?!" Tyler replied. "You're nutty like a fruitcake!"

"What are you talking about?" Colette asked.

By now, I had gotten to my feet again. I was

staring back down the trail, trying to see if there was any movement. It was too dark to tell.

"I'm telling you, I saw a werewolf back there," I repeated, still gasping for breath. "I thought it was Colette, but it wasn't."

"Sure," Brian Ludwig mocked. "A werewolf. Yeah, they're all over the place. You gotta watch out for those werewolves."

"I'm serious, you guys!"

The rest of the group had gathered around. There was Tyler, Colette, Brian, Stuart Lester, James Barker, and me. We all live on the same block, just a few houses from one another.

"Jeremy, there's no such thing as werewolves," Colette said. "You probably saw a coyote."

"Hey, if coyotes stand as tall as you on their hind legs, well, then maybe it *was* a coyote," I answered.

"You're making this up," Stuart said.

"Look, you guys," I said. I was getting angry. "I know what I saw. I saw a creature that was about my size. It was standing on its hind legs, just like a human. Except it had hair all over its face, and it had a dog-like nose. And teeth! Man, did that thing have sharp teeth!"

"Was it really ugly?" James asked.

"Yeah!" I replied.

"Nasty looking?"

"Uh-huh."

"So ugly that you thought you would puke?"

"Yes! Exactly!" I said.

"That settles it, then," James said, matter-of-factly. "That was no werewolf . . . that was my *sister!*"

Everyone started laughing, except Colette and me. "Come on, you guys," she said. "Jeremy really saw something. He's not lying."

"No, I'm not," I said.

"Well, then . . . let's go see if he's still there," Tyler suggested.

Silence.

"Yeah," I said. "Unless you guys are chicken."

"I'm not afraid of any werewolf," Stuart said.

"Me neither," James said.

"Doesn't bother me a bit," Brian chimed in.

"Yeah," said Colette. "The six of us will be safe together. Let's go and see."

I pointed my flashlight beam down the trail, and eerie shadows darted and dove.

"We'll follow you," Stuart said, pulling out his own flashlight. Colette turned her flashlight on, and so did Brian, Tyler, and Stuart. We were six kids with six flashlights, heading down a trail that led into the forest.

Looking for a werewolf.

What we didn't know, of course, was that the werewolf was looking for *us*.

We walked down the trail, each of us sweeping our flashlights into the dark forest around us. Bats chittered as they darted through the trees, and I heard the owl hoot again. That's one of the things I like about Madison, Wisconsin, which is where I live. It's a pretty big city, but we live a little ways out, and there are lots of forests and trees right near our neighborhood. Which means that there are plenty of animals, too. You'll see deer and racoons and owls . . . all kinds of wildlife.

But you're not supposed to see werewolves. Werewolves aren't supposed to be real.

"Are you sure you saw a werewolf?" Brian asked, as we trudged along the trail. "I mean . . . couldn't it have been a bear or something?"

I shook my head. "No way," I replied. "I'm telling you guys . . . I know what I saw. Come on, you know me . . . I'm not making this up. I really was scared. That thing was freaky."

"How much farther do we have to go?" James whined. "I'm missing *SpongeBob*, you know."

"Chill out, James," Colette said. "Your dad is probably recording the show, anyway. He likes it more than you do."

"Well, if we don't find the werewolf soon, I'm going to have to bag it for the night," Brian said. "I've got to get up early to go fishing."

"Awww, is the little baby getting tired?" Stuart chided. Brian ignored the comment.

And the trail wound on. By now, it was really dark. There was no moon, but a zillion stars glistened through the trees.

"See?" Stuart said, pointing his thin flashlight

beam up into the air. "It couldn't have been a werewolf. Werewolves only come out when the moon is full."

"That's just an old wives' tale," Tyler said. "Werewolves can come out at any time."

And then I heard something. It was a crunching, a snapping of branches, and the sound wasn't too far away from us. Stuart heard it, and so did Colette.

The six of us stopped in the middle of the trail, listening. The noise had ceased, and all we could hear were the sounds of the forest.

And then:

Crunch. Snap.

We froze stiff. None of us spoke or even moved.

But we didn't hear anything more. There was only silence. Whatever it was, it wasn't moving around much.

Colette leaned toward me and started to whisper. *"Is this the place where you —"*

But her voice was stopped cold by a shrill, new sound.

A howl.

It was long and loud, and it echoed through the forest . . . and there was no mistaking it.

That howl—that awful, screeching wail—wasn't from a dog or an owl. In fact, no human could make a sound like that.

That howl was from a werewolf.

And when we heard the crunching of branches and the snapping of twigs, I knew that we would never get out of the forest alive.

I suppose you think that we turned and ran.

Wrong.

We *flew*. I don't think our feet hit the ground. We turned and sprang so quickly that we bounced off one another, careening down the dark trail like wild banshees. All of us were screaming . . . even Colette, who usually doesn't scream about anything.

We ran and we screamed, we screamed and we ran. We tore through the dark forest, following our flashlight beams as they bounced along the trail, trying to put as much distance between us and the ghastly creature that, no doubt, was hot on our trail. And we didn't stop until we reached the edge of the forest and the safety of streetlights that glowed brightly along our block.

When we reached the street, all six of us collapsed, sitting on the curb and gasping for air. It was a long time before anyone said anything.

"I'm sorry, Jeremy," Tyler said. "I should have believed you."

"Me too," said James. The rest of the group nodded.

"That was the freakiest sound I've ever heard in my life," Brian said between his heaving gasps. "I didn't think we were going to make it out of there. Not alive, anyway."

"That's what I was trying to tell you guys," I said. "Whatever is in those woods . . . whether it's a werewolf or not . . . isn't human."

"You can bet it's not a cartoon, either," Stuart said, which prompted mild laughter from everyone.

"So . . . what do we do now?" Colette said, pulling a lock of hair away from her face.

"I don't know about you guys," James said, "but I'm going to go home and forget the whole thing. I'm going to wake up in the morning, and this whole thing will be a dream. There's no such thing as werewolves, anyway."

We all sat on the curb, catching our breath. Above us, bugs swarmed and darted beneath the pale blue streetlight.

I would have liked to think that James was right. It would have been great to wake up and discover that everything was a dream, that we hadn't even been in the woods playing hide and seek.

But that's not what happened.

Soon, I would discover — with absolute certainty — that what had happened to us was *real*.

And as I sat on the curb that night with my friends, I wondered about werewolves. I wondered if they really did exist. I wondered if I would ever see the creature again . . . and if I wanted to.

I didn't have to wait very long . . . for the werewolf had followed us. Oh, we didn't know it at the time, but the werewolf had crept through the shadows and was watching us at that very moment.

We were safe, of course, because we were under the glow of the streetlight.

But later that night, after I went to bed, I heard a noise outside my window. I got up to investigate . . . and what I saw sends shivers of terror down my spine to this very day.

It was getting late, and we all needed to go home. Thankfully, we all lived close by. No one would have to walk through dark streets or dimly-lit alleys to get home.

I waited until everyone had left . . . except Colette. She sat on the curb, staring up into the night sky.

"Do you think it was a real, live werewolf?" she asked.

"I don't know," I said, shaking my head. "All I know is what I saw. I'm telling you . . . that was the scariest thing I've ever seen in my life. *Ever.*"

"I believe you," she said, looking straight into my eyes. "I really do."

"Thanks," I said. "But now what do we do? I always thought that werewolves were just creatures that were in movies. You know . . . just made-up things. What if they really are *real?*"

Colette shook her head. "I don't know, Jeremy. I don't know what to do."

We were silent for another moment. The only sounds we could hear were big beetles hitting the streetlight above us, the whir of crickets, and the murmur of traffic on the highway a few blocks over.

"We'll figure it out tomorrow," I said.

"Yes, we will," Colette replied. "Jeremy?"

"Yeah?"

"Thanks for being my friend. I mean that."

"Yeah, sure," I replied. Colette stood up, turned, and walked up to the sidewalk. Then she stopped and turned back.

"See you tomorrow," she said with a wave of her hand.

I raised my hand. "Tomorrow," I agreed. Colette turned again, and walked away.

I sat on the curb for a few minutes, listening to the sounds of the night. I wondered if I would hear that strange howl again, that terrible, horrifying screech that we'd heard in the forest.

No. I listened and listened, but I didn't hear a thing.

Finally, I saw our front door open, and the dark shape of Mom appeared. Before she could yell, I hollered out.

"I'm right here, Mom."

"Time to hit the shower, bud," she said. Mom always calls me 'bud'. She closed the screen, but left the door open. Then she was gone.

I stood up and began walking toward the house. When I reached the porch, I stopped.

Something wasn't right.

I couldn't put my finger on it, but there was something that just *wasn't* right. I stood on the porch, wondering what it was . . . until I *knew* what was wrong.

Everything was *too* quiet. Too, *too* quiet.

Moments ago, I heard crickets and bugs and things. Now, the only thing I could hear were a few cars a long ways away.

No other sounds.

And then . . . .

A low, rumbling growl from the bushes. It was hard to hear at first, but it grew steadily louder and louder.

A chill slithered down my spine like a frozen snake. I was too afraid to move, even though I was only a few feet away from the front door.

The growl grew louder, and then I saw the bushes near the end of our yard move. I tried to yell for Mom and Dad . . . but no words came out.

Then, the bushes seemed to explode—and the beast showed himself, charging across the yard and coming toward me at full speed.

Two seconds changed everything.

In the first second, I saw a terrible beast—a werewolf—attacking, coming from the bushes toward me.

In the next second, I realized what I was *really* seeing . . . Tyler's dog, Rufus. Rufus is a big collie with long, thick hair, like Lassie. He was running full bore across the lawn and toward our porch.

"Geez, Rufus," I said, as the dog ran up to me. "You really freaked me out!" I stroked his neck and petted his head. "I'm sure glad that it was you, though, and not that awful werewolf."

Rufus gave a happy bark, then darted across the lawn toward his home.

Sheesh, I thought, smiling and shaking my head. *Scared by an ordinary dog.*

I went into the house. After taking a shower, I went into my bedroom, put my pajamas on, brushed my teeth, and climbed into bed. In no time at all I was asleep.

When I awoke, it was dark. I didn't know what time it was, but I knew that it was still the middle of the night.

But then I realized why I had awoken:

I had heard something.

I didn't know what I had heard, but something had startled me awake.

I sat up in bed and looked out the window. The streetlight lit up the empty road and our yard. Nothing moved, and everything looked calm and peaceful.

I laid back down and closed my eyes—and then I heard it. From far away . . . .

A howl.

The sound sent a layer of ice over my body, and every hair from my head to my toes stood up on end.

Even though I was really spooked, I threw the covers off and leapt out of bed. I walked over to the window to see if I could see anything.

Nothing moved, and there were no more sounds.

Wow, I thought. *It's really out there somewhere.*

I was just about to turn and go back to bed when I saw a movement in the shadows across the street. As I watched, a figure emerged . . . and there was no mistaking what it was.

A werewolf.

I wanted to scream, to yell for help, but I was too afraid. I know that may sound odd, but if you've ever been as afraid as I was at that moment, you'd understand what it's like to be paralyzed by fear. I could only watch as the bizarre creature prowled the dark shadows, peering around bushes and branches.

Suddenly, the creature stopped and turned around. He sniffed the air and looked up into the sky. Then, as if he *knew* I was watching, he turned his head and looked directly at me. There was no doubt that he knew I was there. He was looking right at me!

Without another moment of hesitation, I ducked down beneath the window. My heart was battering in my chest like a mallet.

How had the creature known that I was watching him? Did he really see me, or was he simply looking in my direction?

I remained huddled below the window for a long time, not sure of what I should do.

Should I go wake up Mom and Dad?

No, they'd probably just think that I was having a nightmare, and tell me to go back to bed.

I don't have any brothers or sisters, either, so there was no one else I could wake up. The only thing I could do was stay where I was or go back to bed . . . and I don't think I could stay much longer in the position I was in. My legs were starting to cramp from being bent in the same position for so long. They would start to hurt if I didn't stretch soon.

All right, I thought. *I'm going back to bed. That's all there is to it.*

I stretched out my legs and prepared to stand

up.

What if that werewolf is still out there? I wondered. *What if he's still across the street, standing in the shadows, waiting? What did he want? What was he looking for?*

I had a million questions, and no answers.

But in the next instant, I knew that the werewolf was no longer across the street—for there was an awful scratching sound on the screen, a terrible scraping, and I knew that the creature was here.

The werewolf had come for me!!!

I let out a scream that would have curled your hair. Instead of standing up, I dove to the middle of the room and rolled. Then I scrambled under my bed, still yelling and screaming.

The terrible scratching had stopped, but there was no way I was going to take the time to look. I knew that I'd see the hideous, awful face of the werewolf staring back at me.

My screams and shouts woke up my Mom and Dad, and I could hear them scrambling down the hall.

Thank goodness, I thought. *Mom and Dad heard me! They're coming to help!*

Suddenly, my door swung open and my bedroom light turned on.

"Jeremy?!?!" Mom shouted. *"Where are you?!?!"*

I struggled and squirmed out from beneath my bed.

"What's the matter?" Dad asked. "What happened?"

"A werewolf!" I exclaimed. *"I saw him across the street! Then, he came after me! He was scratching at the window!"*

Mom and Dad looked at the window . . . just as the scratching sound began again!

"That's no werewolf!" Dad said angrily. "That's a bug!"

Sure enough, a big beetle was on the screen. His legs were held fast to the mesh and his wings were going a mile a minute, hitting the wire screen. It really *did* sound like a claw scratching the screen!

"You were just dreaming," Mom said. Dad

turned to go back to bed.

"No! Wait!" I cried. "I really *did* see a werewolf! Over there, on the other side of the street! I saw him earlier, too . . . in the forest! My friends even heard him howl!"

"Jeremy . . . you were *dreaming,*" Dad scolded. "That's all it was. There is no such thing as werewolves." He turned and left.

"I knew you guys wouldn't believe me," I said.

Mom put her hand on my shoulder. She bent over and kissed my head. "I believe you," she said. "If you say you saw a werewolf, that's what you saw. Sleep tight."

Mom left, but I knew that she didn't *really* believe me.

But I know what I saw. I know what I heard in the forest.

A werewolf. There was a werewolf running around our neighborhood!

I turned off my bedroom light and looked out the window one last time.

Nothing. No werewolf . . . nothing.

I climbed back into bed and pulled the covers up to my chin. Soon, I had fallen back to sleep.

The next morning, I was eating a bowl of cereal when the phone rang. Mom answered it.

"Yes, he's right here," she said. She handed me the phone. "It's Colette."

I put down my spoon and took the phone.

"Hi," I said.

"He was here last night, Jeremy!" She sounded panicked.

"What?" I replied.

"Here! Last night! You've got to see this! There are weird footprints all over our yard!"

I didn't even take the time to finish my cereal. I hung up the phone, put my cereal bowl in the sink, and raced out the door. Colette lives only three houses away, so I was at her house in seconds.

She was outside, standing in the grass, inspecting the ground. She saw me coming.

"You've got to see this!" she exclaimed, and she knelt down in the grass.

I ran up to her and kneeled down.

"Right here," she said, pointing.

"Whoah!" I cried out in a hoarse whisper.

It *was* a footprint. Or a track of some sort. It was bigger than my foot—not by much—but it looked more like an animal track than a footprint. And it looked like claws had dug into the soft grass.

"He was here last night," Colette said. "Right in my yard!"

"I know," I replied. "I saw him!"

Colette looked at me. "What?!?! You saw him?!?! Last night?!?!"

I nodded. "Yeah! I woke up . . . actually, I think I was awakened by a howl, like we heard last night . . . and I saw the werewolf in the yard across the street from our house!"

"Tyler's yard?!?!" Colette gasped.

"Yep. I saw the creature in the shadows. He even turned and looked right at me."

"Then what happened?"

"I ducked down under my bedroom window, and waited. When I stood up, he was gone." I didn't tell Colette that I'd been frightened by a beetle at the window.

"This is just plain freaky," she said. "Do you think that it could be a *real* werewolf?"

"What else could it be? I mean . . . I've always thought that werewolves were just made up monsters for the movies. I didn't think there was any such thing as *real* werewolves."

"That howl sure sounded real last night," Colette said, recalling the strange sound that we all heard in the forest at the end of our block.

Down the street, I heard a front door slam closed. Colette and I turned to see Tyler run across his yard. He looked like he was headed across the street to my house.

"Tyler!" I yelled.

Tyler turned his head, saw us, then changed direction. He ran up to us and stopped, huffing and puffing.

"He was in my yard! Last night!" he gasped, kneeling in the grass next to us.

"I know!" I exclaimed. "I saw him! And look!" I pointed to the footprint in the grass.

"That's nothing!" Tyler exclaimed. "Wait 'till you see what I found at the back of my house!"

"What?" Colette and I said in unison.

Tyler shook his head. "I'll show you. Come on!"

Tyler sprang to his feet, and Colette and I did the same. We ran after Tyler and wound around the side of his house to his back yard. He stopped by a picnic table and pointed at the house.

Look at that! he exclaimed.

At first, I didn't see what he was pointing at. Colette and I stepped closer to the house . . . and when we saw what Tyler was talking about, we both gasped in horror.

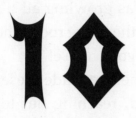

Claw marks.

Beneath Tyler's bedroom window, a series of scratches—claw marks—marred the white vinyl siding. It looked like a dog had ripped into the wall with its paws.

"Holy smoke!" I exclaimed.

"Oh my gosh!" Colette said, drawing a hand over her mouth. "When did you notice it?"

"This morning," Tyler said. "I came out here because Mom asked me to fill up the bird feeder. That's when I saw it."

51

"Didn't you hear anything last night?" I asked.

"Actually, no . . . but Rufus did. He started growling in the living room. I went to see what he was growling at, but I didn't see anything."

"I saw the werewolf in your yard last night!" I told him. "In your front yard! I'll bet that's what Rufus was growling at! I'll bet that when you went into the living room, the werewolf went to the back of your house!"

"That's when he made these scratch marks," Colette agreed, reaching out to the wall. "He came back here and scratched up the wall while you were in the living room." She placed a finger on one of the scrapes. "Whatever made this sure has sharp claws," she finished.

The three of us stood in silence for a moment, staring at the long claw marks on the wall beneath Tyler's bedroom window.

"I didn't think werewolves were for real," Tyler said.

"Me neither," Colette said.

"I didn't, either," I replied. "But I know what I saw last night. That thing was a werewolf."

We searched the grass around Tyler's house for any footprints, but we didn't find any. Probably because the grass in his yard is really thick and cut really short. It would be hard for anyone — ourselves included — to leave any tracks behind.

Finally, the three of us sat down at the picnic table to discuss what we would do.

"This is serious, guys," I said. "I don't know much about werewolves, but I've got to believe that they're dangerous. It won't be long before someone gets hurt."

"Or worse," Colette replied with a shudder.

A noise by the side of the house distracted us, and we turned to see Stuart walking toward us.

The three of us gasped.

Stuart had a large bandage on his arm . . . *and one on his neck!*

11

"What happened?" the three of us asked in unison—but I already knew the answer. Stuart had been attacked by the werewolf . . . or, that's what it *looked* like, anyway. We quickly found out differently.

"I fell in the garage last night," he said sheepishly. "I cut my arm and my neck. I'm lucky that I'm not hurt any worse than I am."

"You mean, you weren't attacked by a werewolf?" I asked.

Stuart frowned. "Of course not," he replied.

55

"Why would you think that?"

We showed him the claw marks on the house, and told him about the footprints in Colette's yard. I told Stuart about what I saw in Tyler's yard last night.

"That's pretty freaky," Stuart said.

"I wonder where he came from," Colette asked. "I mean . . . has he always been around here . . . or is he a real human being that changes into a werewolf at night?"

"It's probably my sister," Stuart said. "She can get pretty ugly sometimes."

Everyone laughed.

"I wonder if anyone else saw anything last night," I said. "I wonder if James or Brian saw the werewolf."

"Only one way to find out," Tyler replied. "Let's go ask them."

Tyler, Colette, Stuart and I got up from the picnic table and set out for Brian's home. He lives only a few houses down the block. On the way, we kept an eye out for anything that seemed out of the ordinary. We were looking for more clues that the werewolf might have left, but we didn't see anything that was out of the ordinary.

The four of us stood on Brian's porch and knocked. Brian's mom came to the door.

"Is Brian around?" Stuart asked.

"Yes, he is. I'll get him." She disappeared and Brian came to the door a few moments later. He stepped outside.

"Hey guys," he said. "What's up? You all look like you've seen a ghost."

"Worse," I replied. "It was a werewolf."

We told him about what I saw in Tyler's yard, the strange footprints at Colette's, and the claw marks beneath Tyler's window.

"We were wondering if maybe you saw or heard anything last night," Colette said.

Brian shook his head. "Not me," he answered. "When I went to bed, I was out like a light."

"You didn't hear any howling or anything?" I asked.

Brian shook his head. "Just the howl that we heard in the forest last night," he replied. "And I think that might have been a dog."

"That was no dog," I disagreed.

"We're going to go over to James' house and see if he knows anything. You want to come?"

"Sure," Brian replied.

The five of us hiked over to James' house. He lives on the same block, but his home is down at the end near the forest . . . however, before we got there, we knew something was really, really wrong.

There was a police car in James's driveway!

The five of us stopped in our tracks. No one said a word, but we were all wondering what could have possibly happened.

"I'll bet he was eaten by the werewolf," Stuart said.

Colette elbowed him in the ribs.

"Ow!" Stuart exclaimed, recoiling.

"He wasn't eaten by a werewolf," I replied.

"You don't know," Stuart answered, rubbing his side.

"Come on," Tyler said, and the five of us

started off toward James's house. We all looked around for evidence that the werewolf had been there, but we didn't see anything.

Finally, we stopped at the curb right in front of James' house. The police car sat in the driveway with its engine running, but there was no one inside. Things seemed pretty quiet.

"Maybe the police are going to take them all to jail," Stuart mused. Colette elbowed him again, and Stuart winced.

Suddenly, the front door opened, and a blue-uniformed police officer came out carrying a coffee mug and a donut. He walked to his car and stopped when he saw us.

"Good morning, guys," he said, raising his coffee cup.

"Good morning," we all replied at once. The policeman popped the donut in his mouth, opened the car door, then grabbed the donut again. He got into the car, backed out of the driveway, and drove off.

"Well, it doesn't look like he was in any big hurry," Colette said.

"Darn," Stuart said. "I thought we were

going to see some action. You know . . . a chase or something." Colette again tried to elbow him, but he dodged her jab.

We walked up to the front door and were greeted by James, who had spotted us and was already on his way outside.

"Hey, guys!" he said.

"Is anything wrong?" Brian asked.

James looked puzzled. "No. Why?"

"Well, we saw the police car here, and we thought that there might be trouble."

James laughed. "Oh, no. No trouble. That guy is a friend of my dad's. He just stopped by to say hello and have a cup of coffee before going to work."

We were all relieved. All but Brian, of course, who was disappointed that he didn't get to see a police chase.

"Did you happen to see anything last night?" I asked. "Because I saw a werewolf in Tyler's yard."

"And there were creepy footprints in my lawn this morning."

"And something scratched up our house, right

beneath my bedroom window," Tyler said.

"As a matter of fact, I did hear something last night," James said. "It sounded like growling. At first I thought it was a dog."

Our eyes beamed.

"What was it?" Colette asked.

"I don't know," James replied. "But I found something in my back yard last night. Hang on."

James disappeared into his house, and the five of us waited anxiously on the porch. He was only gone a few moments, but it seemed like hours.

Finally, he returned, carrying a large paper bag.

"Here," he said, opening up the bag. "I found this in the grass. Take a look."

The five of us peered into the bag.

Colette gasped.

I gasped.

Brian's eyes grew to the size of eggs.

What James had found proved—beyond any shadow of a doubt—that a monster was on the loose.

Werewolf fur.

That's what James had found in his yard. A big clump of long, brown fur.

Werewolf fur.

Tyler let out a whistle and carefully reached into the bag. He pulled out the clump of hair and held it up.

"Werewolf hair!" he exclaimed, and we all reached out to feel it. The hair was long and coarse and felt like strands of sandpaper.

"Couldn't this hair be from a dog?" Stuart

asked, feeling the fur between his fingers.

"Not any dog that I know," I replied. "The hair is too long. This looks like it came from a monster."

"Show us where you found it," Colette said.

"Back here," James replied. "Follow me."

Tyler put the fur into the grocery bag, and we followed James around the side of his house and into his back yard. He took us to a spot near a row of shrubs that grew by the back fence.

"Right here," he said, pointing to the ground. "I found the hair this morning."

We searched the ground around the shrubs, and even the shrubs themselves, but we didn't find anything.

"That settles it," Stuart said. "There's a werewolf on the loose."

"Or two or three," I replied. "If there's one, there might be more."

"It sure looks that way," Tyler said. "Question is . . . what are we going to do about it?"

"I say we call the police," Brian said.

"I say we tell our parents," Colette offered.

"I say we find out a little bit more before we do anything," I said. "Otherwise, we might look pretty silly if we tell everyone that there is a werewolf—or were*wolves*—running loose."

"Yeah, but we have the proof," Stuart piped up. "There are tracks in Colette's yard."

"And claw marks on Tyler's house," Colette said, "not to mention the hair that you found, James."

I shook my head. "We still don't have any proof. I know what I saw last night—both in the forest and in Tyler's yard. But anybody we tell is just going to think that we're a bunch of crazy kids making up stories. We need proof. We need a picture."

"How are we going to get a picture of a werewolf?" Brian asked.

"We go werewolf hunting," Tyler said.

I nodded. "Tyler's right," I said. "We need to find the werewolf. Tonight, after dark. Has everybody got a camera with a flash that they could use?"

Everyone nodded.

"Good. Then let's meet at my house just

before it gets dark. Cool?"

Again, everyone nodded.

"Okay then," I said. "Wear dark clothes, and bring your cameras."

That settled it. We were going werewolf hunting. I figured with the six of us together, we'd be safe.

I was wrong.

I mowed our lawn later in the morning, and then I had some work to do for Mom in the back yard. When I was finished, I went over to Colette's house. She was just returning from a bike ride.

"Do you want to go to the library with me?" I asked.

"Sure," she replied. "What for?"

"I want to find out more about werewolves," I said. "I'll bet they have books about them."

The library was only a few blocks away, so we walked there.

"What are you hoping to find out?" Colette asked me as we walked up the library steps.

I shrugged. "I don't really know," I said. "But I think we should find out what we can before we go looking for one. You know . . . just in case."

"Just in case what?" Colette asked as I opened the door. We walked into the library.

"Just in case we run into trouble," I said.

Our library has a computer system that helps you locate books, but I didn't find any listing for books about werewolves.

"Let's go ask the librarian," I said, and we walked up to the front desk. Mrs. Owens is the librarian . . . but she wasn't there today. In her place was a tall man that I didn't recognize. He seemed busy, and he spoke to us without turning his eyes from his work.

"May I help you," he asked.

"Yeah," I replied. "I was hoping that you might have some books about werewolves."

Suddenly, he stopped what he was doing and looked directly at us. "I beg your pardon?" he said.

"Werewolves," Colette answered. "We were hoping that you'd have some books about werewolves. We didn't find any listed in the computer."

He paused and studied us.

"Why do you want to know about werewolves?" he asked suspiciously.

Colette started to speak. "We saw one last—"

"—school project," I said, interrupting Colette. "We have to do a report for school."

Again, the librarian studied our faces. He was starting to give me the creeps.

"Where is Mrs. Owens?" I asked.

"This is her day off. I'm filling in for her. And yes . . . we *do* have books about werewolves, but we don't have them listed in the computer system yet. Follow me."

The man came around from the desk, and we followed him as he wound around bookshelves and desks. He stopped at one shelf, peering at the books.

"Yes, yes, here we are," he said. "We have quite a few books about werewolves. Help yourselves."

"Thank you," I said.

The man said nothing as he turned and walked away.

"He was kind of strange," Colette whispered.

"Yeah, he was kind of freaky. Come on . . . let's have a look at some of these books."

We spent nearly an hour poring over books about werewolves. There was a lot of history about where they came from, but most of it was theory. None of the books had any proof that werewolves existed. We found a book that had a lot of reported sightings and even a few pictures, but the pictures didn't look real. Plus, they were really blurry.

Colette and I were standing by the shelf. She had just picked out another book when she stopped and touched my arm.

"Jeremy," she whispered frantically. *"That librarian . . . he's . . . he's watching us!"*

I turned and looked over at the librarian's desk.

"No," Colette said. *"Over there! He's on the other side of the bookshelf. It looks like he's spying on us!"*

I turned my head, and sure enough—when I looked over, I saw the librarian's icy glare. When he saw me look his way, he turned his head and pretended to be searching for a book.

"Let's get out of here," I whispered to Colette. She returned the book to the shelf, and the two of us left.

"That guy gave me the creeps," Colette said as we left the library. "I hope we don't come across him again."

But we would. Later that night, we would see the librarian again . . . we just didn't know it yet.

Everyone met at my house just before dark.

"Did everybody bring their cameras?" I asked. Stuart, Colette, Brian, James, and Tyler raised their cameras.

"I even brought my dad's super-power flashlight," Tyler said, holding up a black, coffee-can sized unit.

"I've got one, too," said James.

"And I can get one of ours," I said. "That way, we can divide up into pairs. We'll have a better chance of seeing the werewolf . . . and

73

getting pictures . . . if we split up."

"What if there's more than one werewolf?" James asked.

"There might be," I said. "After all, there's not a lot that we know. We'll just have to be careful. Hang on . . . I'll be right back."

I retrieved a flashlight from my house and met the rest of the group waiting on the porch.

"Everybody ready?" I asked. Everyone nodded.

"James and I will go together," Stuart said.

"Tyler and I will, too," Brian said.

Colette would go with me.

"Where are we going to look first?" Brian asked.

I pointed to where the forest met the road at the end of our block. In the fading light, it looked spooky . . . especially tonight. Beyond the tree line, a bright orange moon was rising.

A *full* moon.

"Everybody set?" I asked. Everyone nodded. "Good. Let's head out."

No one spoke as we walked down the street and headed for the forest, which seemed darker and creepier than ever. The full moon was rising even higher, and it's light was bright enough to create shadows.

In the forest, however, it would be different. In the forest, the light of the moon wouldn't be able to penetrate through the thick trees, and it would be darker than dark.

If I was a werewolf, that's where I'd be.

In the dark of the forest, beneath the full moon.

We reached the edge of the woods and stopped. Crickets chimed peacefully from the shadows. A bat flitted above us and spun into the forest.

"Come on," I said, and the six of us headed for the trail.

None of us were sure if we would actually see the werewolf, or even get a picture.

One thing was for certain, though:

Tonight would be a night that the six of us wouldn't soon forget.

Tyler led the way into the forest and onto the trail, because he had his dad's super-bright flashlight. Our plan was to hike back to a small field where we could split into pairs and search the various trails that wound through the woods. We all knew the trails well, so we weren't worried about getting lost. We'd played lots of games of hide and seek in these woods. Plus, the forest isn't very big, anyway. You couldn't walk too far in any direction without coming out to a street or a group of houses.

No, we weren't worried about getting lost, and we weren't afraid of the dark.

We were afraid of what was *in* the dark.

It didn't take us long to reach the field. Here, the trees fell away, and the full moon hung in the dark sky like a giant light bulb. Zillions of stars speckled the heavens.

An owl suddenly hooted, and Brian jumped.

"Great," Tyler said. "If you're spooked by an old owl, what's going to happen if you spot a werewolf?"

"I wasn't scared," Brian shot back. "It just surprised me."

"Okay, let's split up," I said. "We'll meet back here in thirty minutes, unless anyone has to be home any earlier."

"Not me," said Tyler.

"Nope," James said.

"I'm no baby," Stuart offered.

"I can stay out longer if I want," Brian said.

"As long as I'm home by nine thirty," Colette said.

"Good. Let's go find our werewolf."

James and Stuart took the trail to the south

that wound around a big swamp, while Brian and Tyler crossed the field and followed a trail north. Colette and I took the trail that led to the place I had been hiding the night before . . . the place where I had spotted the werewolf. I carried my flashlight in one hand and a camera in the other. Colette held her camera at the ready, with her finger on the button. If we were surprised by a werewolf, she wanted to make sure she'd get a picture.

Branches crunched beneath our feet as we made our way deeper into the woods. The owl hooted a few times, only this time it was farther away. We caught a glimpse of the moon through scrambled tree branches.

But we didn't see or hear anything except the normal things you would expect from the forest at night. Colette and I were quiet as we trudged along. Then we stopped when we reached the place where I had spotted the werewolf the night before.

"This is right where I saw him," I said, sweeping the flashlight beam through branches and limbs. *"I was hiding right over there . . . and the werewolf*

was right over . . . there."

But tonight, there was nothing there but trees and shrubs.

"I wonder if anyone else has had any luck tonight," Colette whispered.

And they were. Or, perhaps it wasn't *luck* at all . . . because right after Colette had finished speaking, the night was shattered by a terrible scream, deep in the forest.

A scream that sounded like Stuart!

17

"That was Stuart!" I exclaimed. "I'm sure of it!"

We spun on the trail and jogged as fast as we could without tripping over branches or stumbling over exposed roots. Our flashlight beams bounced and tumbled, and eerie shadows darted away like bashful ghosts.

Colette and I were the first to reach the field. Panting and out of breath, we stopped and listened.

"I couldn't tell where that scream came from," Colette said.

I shook my head. "Me neither. We'll wait here for a few minutes. If no one shows up, we'll go looking."

The bright moon looked down upon us like a silvery eye, watching us as we stood and waited. No more sounds came from the forest, except for the soft whirring of crickets. Even the owl had stopped hooting.

Suddenly, we heard branches snapping and popping. I trained my flashlight into the forest in the direction of the noise, until I saw two shadows moving.

Brian and Tyler.

They hurried up to us in the field, their legs swishing in the tall grass.

"Did you hear the scream?" Colette asked.

"I think it was Stuart!" Brian exclaimed. "He screamed once, and that was it. We didn't hear anything else."

"We didn't, either," I said. "I hope he's all right."

"What do we do?" Tyler asked. "Should we go look for him?"

"No," I replied. "Let's hang on a minute. If

Stuart and James don't show up soon, we'll go look for them."

And so we waited. I kept glancing down at my watch, which I could see clearly in the light of the moon. With every passing minute, we became more and more worried.

A branch cracked, and we held our breath. Then another.

"Do you think it's them?" Colette asked.

No one had to answer her. In the next instant, we heard James' scolding voice echoing though the forest.

"Why don't you watch where you're going?!?!"

"I couldn't see!" Stuart replied.

"Yeah, and who's fault is that?!?!?"

Whew. They were safe.

"Hey guys!" I shouted. "Over here!" I pointed my flashlight beam in the direction of the sounds they were making. Soon, two shadows came into view.

"Are you guys all right?" Tyler asked. "We heard a scream. It sounded like *you*, Stuart."

"Oh, it was him all right," James replied. "Captain Werewolf Hunter got freaked out . . . by a raccoon!"

"Hey, the thing surprised me!" Stuart said, trying to defend himself. "And he came after me!"

"He did not!" James corrected. "He was more afraid of you than you were of him. He just wanted to get away from us as quickly as he could. You screamed because you thought he was attacking you."

"Never mind," I said. "Did you guys see anything else? Any signs of a werewolf?"

"No, we didn't see a thing. Did you?"

Colette shook her head. "We went back to the spot where Jeremy saw the werewolf last night," she said. "But there was nothing there. How about you, Tyler?"

"Brian and I didn't see a thing," he answered.

Rats. Our werewolf hunting trip had been unfruitful.

I looked at my watch. "Well, it's getting late. We'd better head back."

We hiked back along the trail and headed back to the street. I was really kind of bummed. I'd really hoped that we'd spot a werewolf, and be able to take a picture. Then we would have proof.

"Some werewolf hunters we turned out to be," Colette said as we reached the end of the forest. In front of us, the neighborhood opened up. Windows in houses glowed, and streetlights lit up the streets.

"Well, maybe tomorrow night," I said hopefully.

But tonight wasn't over yet. Not by a long shot.

We had just emerged from the forest. The six of us were chattering to one another as we headed for the sidewalk . . . when Tyler suddenly stopped and froze. We all noticed it, and we turned to see what he was looking at.

A block away, beneath a streetlight, stood not one . . . but *two* werewolves!

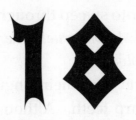

Six kids gasped beneath a full, shiny moon. There was no mistaking what we were seeing beneath the streetlight at the end of the block.

Werewolves.

They stood up on their hind legs, side by side, looking at us.

Glaring at us.

They had hair all over their arms and faces. And they were wearing clothes! Both creatures had ratty jeans and shirts that looked old and torn.

And their *ears*. They had long, pointy ears, the kind of ears you would expect to see on a werewolf.

I was terrified, and I knew that Colette, Stuart, James, Tyler, and Brian were, too. It was like the air we were breathing had become filled with fear, and each breath we drew caused another wave of horror to sweep through our bodies.

It was real! It was true! There really is such a thing as werewolves!

I could almost see their tongues flicking over their razor-sharp teeth. Although I was too far away to see their eyes, I was certain that they probably glowed red or yellow.

And then—

They moved. They turned and darted and began to run, out of the street and into a yard.

"The cameras!" I hissed. *"Get your cameras! Get a picture!"*

We had been so freaked out by seeing the werewolves beneath the streetlight that we'd forgotten the purpose of our expedition was to get a picture of a werewolf . . . and by the time any of us had our cameras up and ready to shoot, the strange creatures had darted into the shadows.

"Let's go!" I shouted, and I started to run. I heard footsteps behind me as the rest of the group followed.

"I can't believe we're chasing werewolves," James huffed.

"I can't believe there really is such a thing as werewolves," Colette panted.

It only took a couple seconds to reach the place where the two werewolves had been standing. I chugged to a halt, frantically searching the gloomy shadows for any movement.

"Which way did they go?!?" Stuart asked.

I pointed into the shadows between two houses. "Over there, I think!" I said, training my flashlight beam into the darkness. "I think they went that way!"

Cameras ready, we jogged across the lawn, flashlights blazing ahead of us. We stopped in between the two houses.

"Look for tracks," I said, pointing my flashlight at the dewy grass. We spent the next few minutes searching.

And then:

"Right here!" Tyler squealed. *"There are werewolf tracks in the grass!"*

We gathered around. Sure enough, we could make out depressions in the grass where the werewolves had been.

"Those are the same kind of tracks that were in my yard this morning!" Colette said.

"Where do they lead to?" Brian asked.

I aimed my flashlight beam in the direction that I thought the werewolves had fled. "Over that way," I replied. "Through that dark yard over there."

"Let's follow them!" Tyler chirped.

"Yeah, lets!" Colette agreed.

I shined my flashlight onto my watch. "We only have a few minutes left," I said. "It's getting late. I have to be home soon, and so do you guys. Everyone in favor of following the tracks for a few minutes, say 'aye'."

"Aye," everyone said in unison.

The matter was settled. We would follow the tracks, at least for a few minutes, to see where they went.

90

And I will say this:

If you get scared easily, don't read any further. Put this book down ... because what was about to happen would scare the daylights out of anyone.

We knew we didn't have long before we'd have to go home, so we got right down to business. Tyler, who had his dad's really powerful flashlight, led the way, aiming the beam at the ground and following the tracks in the grass. We knew that we couldn't be far from the werewolves.

We walked in a single file line, one right after the other. And we walked close to each other, too. I don't think anyone wanted to get too far away from the group.

The tracks led through several dark back

yards, and we thought we lost the trail when the tracks seemed to end at a street. But Tyler was able to pick up the prints on the other side of the road, so we continued. We followed the tracks as they wound behind houses and through yards, all around the block . . . and ended at the forest.

The same forest that we had been werewolf hunting earlier in the night!

We stopped. Tyler swept the flashlight beam into the dark woods.

"I can't go in there," Colette said. "Not tonight. It's getting late, and I have to be home real soon."

"Same here," said James.

I was kind of disappointed. I'd really hoped that we were on to something. That maybe the tracks would lead us to the werewolves.

"Yeah," I said, "you guys are right. Maybe tomorrow night we'll have another chance."

I spoke too soon.

All at once we heard a crash, like the violent sound of a bunch of branches crunching. The sound came from the forest, and it was close by.

"What is it?!?!" Stuart hissed.

Tyler's flashlight beam jumped and darted, and finally focused on the area where the noise was coming from.

Every single one of us screamed. We screamed . . . and we ran. No one took the time to take pictures. No one wanted to.

It was the two werewolves. Only now, they weren't running away from us . . . they were charging right for us, their teeth-filled jaws chomping, and their sharp claws raised above their heads.

And even as I turned and fled, I knew that there was no way we would be able to outrun them.

The six of us began running so fast that we bumped into one another. Colette fell, and I helped her up. All the while we were screaming and yelling like howling banshees.

But there was other howling, too.

Behind us, the two werewolves charged. They were snarling and howling like wild, crazy animals . . . and they were getting closer.

I wasn't going to waste time by looking behind me. I knew that the two werewolves were hot on our tail, and if I turned to look I might fall.

Instead, I concentrated on running as fast as I possibly could, heading for a bright streetlight up ahead that was in front of my house. I was sure that, once we were out in the open, someone would hear our screams and come to help.

However, I knew that all of us wouldn't make it. I knew that I probably would, because I'm a fast runner. So is Colette and Stuart. Brian is pretty fast, and so is Tyler . . . but James runs like a turtle. I knew that he wouldn't have a chance to outrun two vicious werewolves.

We were halfway up the block. I could hear the werewolves behind us, getting closer and closer by the second.

And I could hear James screaming and screeching.

"Ahhhhhh!! Don't let them get me!! Don't let them get meeeeeeeee!"

"You can do it, James!" I managed to shout. *"Keep running! You can do it!"*

We were almost under the streetlight, running up the sidewalk, our feet thundering on the cement. Colette was at my side, keeping stride with me, while Stuart raced at my heels.

All the while, the terrible growls and howls of the werewolves kept getting closer and closer and closer — until finally, the unthinkable happened.

There was a loud howl and a snarl. Then James screamed an agonizing, terrible wail.

"Aaaaahhhhhh! It's got me . . . It's — "

His voice fell silent, cut short.

It had happened. The werewolves were simply too fast . . . and James had just become their first victim.

I couldn't run any more. I mean . . . I probably could, but I wouldn't. Not with James in trouble—and he was in a lot of it.

I stopped and turned, and so did Colette. Stuart almost ran into me, but missed at the last instant. He tumbled on past, and then he, too, stopped and turned.

The werewolves had indeed attacked, taking down James.

There was no time to lose.

"Come on!" I shouted. "We've got to stop

them! We've got to save James!"

I didn't know what we were going to do. How do you fight a werewolf? What would we use? I know that garlic is supposed to keep vampires away, but I didn't think it would work with werewolves. I remember seeing a movie where a werewolf was stopped by a silver bullet—but where would we get one of those?

By now, both werewolves were on top of James. They were thrashing and pawing and clawing. I could hear them snarling and howling as they assailed James, and it only made me run faster.

Colette and Stuart were right behind me, and Brian and Tyler were right behind them. There were five of us—not including James, of course—so maybe we had a chance. At least we outnumbered the hairy beasts.

Ahead of me, the werewolves continue to roll over James, their howls and snarls echoing down the street. James was screaming like crazy. Sooner or later, other people would hear his cries for help. They'd hear the terrible growls and bellows from the werewolves, and they'd come to help.

But then it might be too late.

I was ready to dive into the tangled mass of flailing creatures when, all of a sudden, I heard a different sound.

Laughter.

Not just any laughter—James' laughter! He was trying to speak!

"Hey! Hahahah! Knock it off! Ahahahah! Hey! That tickles!"

One of the werewolves rolled sideways in the grass, laughing and howling. The other werewolf still held James to the ground.

"Hey!" James shouted. *"Stop tickling me!"*

There was something fishy here, all right!

Just as I was about to leap and pounce on the werewolf that had attacked James, it rolled sideways into the grass.

Now I had a chance. The creature was looking the other way, and I attacked with all of my weight, landing flat on top of the werewolf.

"Ooooof!" cried the werewolf as I knocked the wind from him.

Stuart was now at my side and he joined the

scuffle as well.

The second werewolf now leapt into the action, followed by Colette and Stuart, then Brian and Tyler. Even James re-joined the action as we tried to hold down the fighting creatures.

Suddenly, we heard a voice that we didn't recognize.

"Owww!! Cut it out! We were only playing around!"

Talking werewolves?!?!

It was then that I noticed something about the werewolves's faces, and I reached down and grabbed one by the chin. I gave a heavy tug—and the face of the werewolf came off!

It was a mask!

They weren't werewolves . . . they were kids like us, only a little bit older . . . wearing *masks!*

I let go of him and stood up. I was breathing hard and my chest was heaving. Stuart got to his feet, then Colette, then James and Brian and Tyler. The 'werewolf' that I had pulled the mask from stood up, and the one that was still wearing his mask threw up his arms, tilted his head back, and gave a long, loud howl.

"What's going on here?!?!" I demanded. "What do you guys think you're doing?!?!"

"Scaring the daylights out of *you!*" the unmasked kid said to me, pointing.

Now, the other kid pulled his mask off. "Yeah," he said. "And it worked. You guys were crying like babies!"

"We were *not!*" Colette protested angrily.

"You guys were scared, and you know it," one of the older kids said. "We set up everything *perfectly.*"

"What do you mean by that?" Tyler asked. "What do you mean you 'set things up'?"

"By leaving fake footprints in the grass," the other kid said. "And fake fur by the bushes."

"But the claw marks at your house were the *best,*" the other kid said. "We knew that would freak you guys out. Plus, these masks and fake claws we got at the costume store are awesome!" He pulled one of his gloves off. The entire mitt went all the way up his arm, and it was covered with long, furry hair. The claws were long and curled, capped with plastic fingernails. It looked very real.

"I don't think it's so funny," James said.

"Me neither," Brian and Stuart agreed.

"Yeah," one of the werewolves sneered. "That's because you're just a bunch of punky kids. Come on, Phil. Let's go scare some other brats on another block."

And with that, the two kids put their masks back on. One of them let out another long, shrieking howl, and they started running. They ran down the block and finally disappeared around a dark corner.

"Well, they sure fooled me," Brian said.

"Me, too," agreed Stuart.

"They fooled all of us," I said. "I have to admit, they really had *me* believing that there were *real* werewolves on our block."

We heard a noise, and we all turned toward Tyler's house. His mom's shadow appeared in the doorway.

"Tyler?" she called out. "Time to come in."

"I gotta go, guys," he said. "I'll see you tomorrow." Tyler turned and sprinted toward his house.

"Yeah, me too," said James, who was still

pulling grass out of his hair and off of his shirt.

"Guess I better run, too," Stuart said, and both he and Brian headed for home. Only Colette and I remained.

"Man, they really had me fooled," I said.

"Me too," Colette replied. "They sure looked real. I guess we should have known better. We should have known that there's no such things as werewolves."

I glanced at my watch. It was getting late.

"Well, good night," I said. "I'll see you tomorrow. Want to go fishing down by the creek?"

But Colette wasn't listening. *"Jeremy . . . look."* Her voice was a hoarse whisper, and she sounded concerned. I turned to look where she was pointing, and a shiver crept down my spine.

A block away, standing in the shadows of a large tree, was a man.

Not a *kid* . . . but a *man.* He was just standing there, looking at us.

And right away, we knew who it was.

"It's him!" Colette hissed. *"It's that creepy librarian that was watching us today!"*

Suddenly, the man was gone, vanishing into the shadows.

One strange mystery had been solved . . . but now, the real horror was about to begin.

22

The next morning, Colette, Tyler and I went to the library. We had to find out more about the creepy librarian, and I was certain that Mrs. Owens would know more about him.

"He was really strange," Colette explained to Tyler while we walked. The day was sunny and bright, and we all had to squint our eyes in the harsh light. "He wanted to know why we were interested in werewolves," Colette continued. "Then we caught him spying on us when we were going through books. He gave me the creeps."

"What was he doing when you saw him last night?" Tyler asked.

"We don't know," I said, shaking my head. "He was just standing there, in the shadows, watching us. I don't know how long he had been there."

"That's weird," Tyler said. "I wonder if he's a werewolf."

"That's silly," Colette insisted. "Librarians can't be werewolves."

"Says who?" Tyler replied.

"Well . . . they just can't," Colette answered. "Besides . . . who ever heard of a librarian werewolf?"

We arrived at the library just after it opened. I was first inside, followed by Colette, then Tyler. We looked around at the empty tables.

"There's no one here yet," Colette said quietly. *"We must be the only ones here."*

"Except for Mrs. Owens," Tyler replied quietly. *"She's got to be here somewhere."*

"Probably in her office," I whispered. *"Come on. Let's go find her. She probably can tell us more about the guy that filled in for her yesterday."*

110

Mrs. Owens wasn't in her office. In fact . . . the light wasn't even on.

Strange.

"She's got to be around here somewhere," I said. *"Come on. Let's go look for her. She's probably returning books to the shelves."*

We have a pretty big library—two entire floors—and it took a few minutes of searching.

But we still didn't find her.

"This is too weird," Colette said. The three of us were standing at the main entry of the library. I looked at my watch.

"It's almost eleven o'clock," I said. *"Mrs. Owens isn't here, there are no other people here, and the front door is open. Something really freaky is going on."*

"Well," Colette said quietly to Tyler, *"as long as we're here, we might as well show you what we found out about werewolves. Come on."*

We turned to walk over to the shelves with the books about werewolves . . . but we didn't get very far.

The librarian . . . the man who had filled in for Mrs. Owens . . . was standing in front of the shelf that held the books about werewolves.

And he was smiling. He was holding a book, and smiling. While we watched, he flipped open the book, leafed through the pages —

And began to change!

We watched in horror as hair began to grow on his face, his arms, his hands. His nose grew, and so did his teeth. Still, he kept flipping the pages of the book. Soon, hair covered every exposed area of his skin.

"Oh . . . oh . . . my . . . my . . . gosh!" Colette stammered.

Then, the librarian/werewolf tilted his head back and let out an unearthly howl. He placed the book on the table and started walking toward us.

The three of us didn't have to say a thing to one another. We didn't have to plan anything, didn't have to scream.

We were getting out of there.

Now.

We all spun at the same time. Thankfully, we were right by the front door.

Tyler reached it first. He grabbed the handle — but the door didn't budge!

"*It's . . . it's locked!*" he shrieked, trying to pull the door. "*I . . . I can't get it open!*"

Behind us, the weirdo librarian/werewolf kept walking toward us. He was moving slowly, patiently, like he knew we couldn't get away.

"*Open the door, Tyler!*" Colette screamed.

"*I can't!*" Tyler screeched in terror. "*We're locked in! Someone locked us in!*"

The three of us frantically pulled at the door, but it wouldn't budge. Somehow, the door had been locked.

And behind us, the librarian/werewolf began to speak. His voice was low and deep, a raspy, rumbling snarl.

"*No, children,*" he began, "*there is no escape. None at all. You are mine now, and you will become like me. You three will soon know what it feels like to howl at the moon, to lurk in the shadows, to run with the night. You will soon know what it is like . . . to be a werewolf.*"

We began screaming as loud as we could, and pounding on the glass door. Outside, on the street, people were walking by. If we could only get their attention!

We kept pounding and pounding and screaming. The pounding sounded like thunder in my head, but I could hear the beast coming from behind, taking his time, knowing that we couldn't escape.

Pound-pound-pound. Our fists pummeled the doors. *Pound-pound-pound.*

"*It's too late, children,*" the librarian/werewolf said.

I spun. The creature was right behind us, his arms outstretched, his claws reaching for us.

"*Prepare yourselves, children,*" he said. "*Prepare yourselves . . . to become werewolves!*"

The pounding in my ears suddenly grew louder.

"*No!*" I shouted. "*I don't want to be a werewolf!*"

"Jeremy?" a new voice said. "Wake up, Jeremy . . . you're dreaming."

Mom!

I opened my eyes. Early morning sunlight was coming through my bedroom window. My sheets were all over the bed, like I had been struggling.

The door was open, and Mom was peeking in.

"Colette is on the phone," she said.

I swung my legs over the side of the bed and shook my head. The dream—or nightmare, rather—had really shaken me. It seemed so real.

But I sure was glad that it was *only* a dream!

I got out of bed and walked out of my room and into the kitchen. Mom handed me the phone.

"Hello?"

"Hey. It's me."

"Hi, me," I said.

"Funny. Hey. I have an idea. Let's go to the library this morning and ask Mrs. Owens about that creepy guy."

I cringed, remembering my dream.

It was just a nightmare, I reminded myself. *That's all it was. A nightmare.*

"Um, yeah, okay," I said. "What time?"

"Meet me at my house at ten," Colette replied. "And wait until I tell you about the dream that I had last night!"

"Huh?" I answered.

"Yeah," she said, laughing. "I dreamed that the guy at the library really *was* a werewolf! Isn't that silly?"

"Yeah," I said, nervously. "That's silly."

"Well, I gotta go. See you in a little while." There was a click, and Colette was gone.

I hung up the phone.

Wow, I thought. *Colette dreamed that the librarian was a werewolf! What if she had the same dream that I had?*

No. That was impossible. She must have had a different dream. There's no way she could have had the same dream that I did.

I started trying to piece together bits and pieces of what we knew, and the more I thought about it, the more I began to think that something really *was* going on. I mean . . . we had been tricked by those other kids, that was for sure. We all thought that there were *real* werewolves in the neighborhood.

But now we had another mystery:

Just who was the part-time librarian . . . and why had he been watching us last night? What did he want?

I wasn't sure if I wanted to know.

I met Colette at her house at ten o'clock,

sharp. The mid-morning sun was already hot, and I knew that the day was going to be another scorcher.

"Ready?" she asked.

"Let's go," I answered, and we began walking to the library.

"Tell me about your dream," I said.

"Oh yeah," she began. "It was freaky. I dreamed that you and Tyler and I went to the library to find out more about the weird guy . . . but he locked us inside the library and turned all three of us into werewolves."

I stopped on the sidewalk and gasped. "You're kidding!?!" I exclaimed.

Colette shook her head. "No. No, I'm not. That was my dream."

"Colette . . . that was my dream, too. I had the exact same dream that you had!"

We walked in silence the rest of the way to the library. I couldn't believe that Colette had had the same dream that I had. She couldn't believe that her dream was the same as mine, either.

The library was open, and I saw people going in and out. Colette and I walked up the steps and strode inside. Mrs. Owens was at her desk, and she recognized us instantly.

"Hello Jeremy, hi Colette," she said, smiling. "What can I do for you on this fine morning?"

"A lot, we hope," Colette replied. "We were

hoping you could tell us more about that guy that was here yesterday."

Mrs. Owens looked puzzled.

"You know . . . the guy who filled in for you yesterday. The part-time librarian."

"Media Specialist," Mrs. Owens corrected. "He's a part-time *Media Specialist*. What about him?"

"Well . . . we just wanted to know more about him," Colette said. "You know . . . like where he's from, stuff like that. We've never seen him around here before."

Mrs. Owens's face tightened with concern. She knelt close to us and glared into our eyes.

"Let me tell you this, children," she whispered quietly. Her voice was strong, almost scolding. *"You stay away from him. He was sent to work here to help me. Well, I don't need his help. There's something odd about him. I don't know what it is. He might be — "*

Mrs. Owens stopped speaking and looked around cautiously, making sure that no one else was listening.

" – he might be dangerous," she continued. *"I*

don't know much about him, but I would stay away from him if I were you." She glared at us, and she almost looked . . . mean. *"Do you understand? Be careful if you're ever around him. I wouldn't trust him."*

Colette and I nodded, and Mrs. Owens backed away. She smiled sweetly. "Was there anything else?"

"No," I answered. "That's all. We had a feeling that he was a creepy guy. Thanks for the warning."

Mrs. Owens smiled again, and began filing papers that were on her desk.

"Come on, Colette," I said, and we turned and left.

"I told you something wasn't right about that guy," Colette said.

"Hey, you don't have to tell me," I said. "I knew that he was freaky the moment I saw him spying on us."

We walked down the steps of the library and onto the sidewalk.

"Even Mrs. Owens doesn't like him," I said. "And Mrs. Owens likes *everybody*."

No sooner had I spoken those words when a voice from the library parking lot called out to us. Colette and I both turned . . . and instantly, we both froze in fear.

The creepy librarian guy. He was standing in the parking lot, calling out to us.

"Hey, you two," he said. "I want to talk to you."

The dream that I'd had the night before came back to me. In my mind, I could see the man growing hair and long ears and teeth.

"What do we do?" Colette hissed.

"We run, that's what we do," I replied. And without another thought, Colette and I sprang. We raced side by side down the sidewalk toward home.

Colette shot a glance over her shoulder.

"Oh no!" she cried. *"He's chasing us! He's coming after us, Jeremy!"*

I whipped my head around, only for an instant, and caught a glimpse of the strange man. He was after us, all right . . . and he was a lot faster than we were!

"We won't be able to outrun him!" I shouted, still running at breakneck speed. *"He's too fast! He runs like a —"*

Werewolf. I didn't say it, but I knew that Colette understood.

"Quick! This way!" Colette huffed, turning around a corner and darting through a thick row

of shrubs. She disappeared, and I followed. Branches smacked at my face and I almost tripped. In the next instant, I was in someone's back yard.

"Duck down!" Colette hissed, falling to the grass and rolling behind the shrubs. I hit the ground next to her in a heaping clump. *"Maybe we can fool him,"* she said. *"Maybe he'll think we rounded the corner and ran into a house or something!"*

Both of us were on our stomach, hunched down in the bushes, waiting.

We didn't have to wait long. Seconds later, we heard pounding footsteps getting closer and closer. Then we saw a pair of legs whir past. They went around the corner, slowed, then stopped. He was so close we could hear him breathing. Suddenly, he shouted.

"I don't know where you are," he yelled, *"but I'll find you! I'll find you!"*

Gulp!

We didn't move. I tried to stop the clanging of my heart, for I was certain that he would hear it banging in my chest. Colette held her hand over her mouth to silence her breathing.

After what seemed like a lifetime, the man turned around and began walking back . . . and as he did, we heard a *splat* sound, like he had dropped something by accident. Whatever it was, it landed on the sidewalk right in front of us — but we couldn't see it through the thick bushes.

We remained on the ground, hidden in the bushes, for a long time . . . just in case. Then I crawled to my knees and poked my head through the bushes.

"All clear," I said to Colette, and I crawled through the shrubs to the sidewalk. Colette followed.

"What did he drop?" she asked.

"I don't know," I said, "but it looks like some kind of book."

And it was.

On the sidewalk was a small book, the size of a paperback. It was old and brown, and the cover looked as if it was made of leather. I reached down and picked it up.

"What's it say?" Colette asked, peering over my shoulder.

"I don't know," I replied, flipping the book over in my hands. The cover was indeed made of leather, and it was really worn. There was no writing on the front or the back, or the spine.

"Open it up," Colette urged. "Let's see what it is."

I opened the cover carefully . . . and what I read on the first page took my breath away.

Colette gasped. I inhaled deeply, so quickly that I nearly choked on my own breath!

I read the words written in bold print on the first page.

"Werewolves of the World," I read.

"You see?!?!?" Colette cried. "We were right! He's a werewolf!"

"Just because he's carrying a book doesn't mean he's a werewolf," I said.

"Yeah, but it's got to mean *something,*" she replied. "I've never seen a book like that. And I doubt he got it at the library."

I opened the book to the table of contents. The pages were brown and yellowed with age. There were some strange chapter titles, but it appeared that the book was some kind of guidebook . . . like an encyclopedia of werewolves.

"It looks like this thing tells all about werewolves," I said. "Like, where they came from. And look at this," I continued, pointing to yet another page. "It looks like different types of werewolves come from different parts of the world."

"So . . . not all werewolves are the same?" Colette asked, still looking over my shoulder.

"Not according to this book," I replied. "But it will take some reading to really understand it."

"Why do you think he has a book like this?" Colette asked. "And why did he want to talk to us?"

"He probably wants to turn us into a werewolf," I replied.

"I'm not kidding," Colette replied sharply.

"I'm not, either," I said sincerely, looking at her. "I'm not kidding at all. This is serious stuff.

If this guy is trying to turn us into werewolves, we need to know why — and *how* — he plans to do it."

"Don't you think we should tell someone?" Colette asked. "Like Mrs. Owens?"

My eyes lit up. "Yeah!" I said. "That's it! Let's go back and tell Mrs. Owens! She would know what to do!"

We walked slowly back to the library, wary that the creepy guy could be anywhere. Thankfully, we didn't see him.

I opened the door, and we strode inside. There were several people seated at desks and browsing bookshelves. Mrs. Owens was in her office.

"Mrs. Owens?" I said, tapping on the side of her office door. She looked up and smiled.

"Yes?" she answered.

"Can we talk to you for a moment?"

"Certainly, children," she said. "Come in."

We walked into her office, and she motioned for us to sit down.

"What can I do for you?" she asked.

"Well, it's about that guy," I said. "You know

. . . that librarian—"

"Media Specialist," Mrs. Owens corrected gently.

"Uh, yeah. Media Specialist. Anyway, we think that, well . . . we think that . . . ."

"What Jeremy is trying to tell you is that we think he's a werewolf," Colette said.

Mrs. Owens drew back, her face twisted in horror. *"A werewolf?!?!"* she exclaimed loudly. Then she turned suddenly, looking around to see if anyone else in the library had heard her.

I nodded. "Yeah," I said. "I know that it's weird and all that, but . . . well . . . there have been some pretty strange things going on. And this kooky guy seems to show up at the strangest places."

"Yeah," Colette replied. "We just saw him in the parking lot. It was like he was waiting for us."

"Did he say anything to you?" Mrs. Owens asked. She was very concerned, and I was glad that she believed us.

"He said that he wanted to talk to us," I replied.

"Tell me, children . . . how many of you have seen this man?"

"Just me and Colette," I said.

Mrs. Owens leaned forward and began speaking very quietly. "Listen carefully. There are some things going on that you do not understand. But one thing is certain. You are both in great danger."

I felt the blood drain from my face. I looked at Colette, and she looked at me. She looked shaken.

"I can't explain it all now," she said. "But you must know. I must tell you everything so you will be able to defend yourself. Come back here tonight when the library is closing, and I will explain everything to you. Do not be late."

A shiver snaked down my spine. I looked at Colette again, and she looked at me.

"Okay," I agreed, and Colette nodded.

"Good. I'll see you tonight. And children?"

"Yes?" Colette and I both replied in unison.

"Stay away from that man. Whatever you do . . . stay away from him."

We said that we would, and then we left.

"Talk about freaky!" Colette replied as we

jogged home. "I wonder what all of this means?"

Well, we would find out, all right. Tonight, we would come face-to-face with a werewolf.

Not some kid in a costume.

Not some fake trick by someone who was just trying to scare us.

But a real, live werewolf.

Yes, I admit, I was afraid—and I would find out that night that I had good reason to be.

Thankfully, there was no sign of the strange guy on our way home.

"Why didn't you show her the book that we found?" Colette asked as we stood in front of our house.

"I want to take it home and read it first," I said. "I want to find out more about this guy, especially if we ever run into him again."

I spent the rest of the day reading that book. I read page after page, and I learned a lot about werewolves. Mostly, I learned that everything I knew about werewolves wasn't true. Most of what I knew about werewolves was just stuff that was made up for the movies.

That day was one of the longest days of my life, just sitting around, reading, waiting, reading more, waiting, reading more. I couldn't wait until the library closed and we met with Mrs. Owens. I just knew that she was going to share some dark secret about werewolves.

Maybe that's why that man was here, after all. Maybe he wanted to turn people into werewolves.

I ate a small lunch and went right back to reading . . . and I made a discovery that I couldn't believe.

I read faster and faster, absorbing the information and learning from what I'd read. I've always liked to read for fun, but today I felt like I needed to read to learn as much as I possibly could as quickly as I could.

And when evening came, I'd read enough. I knew now that something was going to happen tonight. Something freaky.

And I knew that Mrs. Owens was going to

warn us. She was looking out for us, and was going to help us.

I called Colette on the phone and asked her to come over right away. I told her that it was important, and that I had to talk to her before we went to the library.

She raced over, and the two of us sat on the porch of my house.

"You're not going to believe what I found out," I said.

And when I began to explain, her jaw just about dropped to the ground.

"There are many different types of werewolves," I explained to Colette. I had the old book in my hand, and I leafed through several pages. "There are some werewolves that only come out on a full moon, but there are others who don't. They're the most dangerous ones."

"The ones that don't come out on a full moon?" Colette asked.

"That's right. It says in here that there is a type of werewolf that is a human on every day of the year . . . except on nights *after* a full moon. That's the night that it will change from a human into a werewolf. Whoever it bites that night will become a werewolf, just like that creature. And that's the scary part." I looked Colette directly in the eye. "Last night was a full moon."

Colette gasped. "You mean—"

"Yep," I said, nodding. "That creepy librarian guy—"

"Media Specialist," Colette corrected.

"—whatever. He's *that* kind of a werewolf! That's why he wanted to talk to us. He wants to turn us into werewolves! Tonight! Mrs. Owens is going to warn us and help us."

"Wow," Colette whispered. "I can't believe it. This is like something out of my *American Chillers* books!"

"Yeah, but those are just books," I replied. "The guy who writes that stuff just makes it up. "This, on the other hand, is for real . . . and it's happening right here in Madison."

By now, it was growing darker, and the library would be closing soon. Earlier in the day, I couldn't wait for nighttime to come.

Now, I wasn't so sure. After reading more about the different kinds of werewolves there are, I was a little more frightened. So was Colette.

"We'll be fine," I said. "Mrs. Owens won't let anything happen to us. Besides . . . I have a secret weapon." I held up a tiny plastic vial for her to see.

"What's that?" she asked.

"You might say that it's 'werewolf repellant', I replied. "I found out about it in that book."

"What's in it?"

"Just ordinary herbs and spices from Mom's kitchen. They all had to be crushed and mixed perfectly."

"What's it supposed to do?" Colette asked.

"Well, if I mixed everything correctly, it's supposed to stop werewolves. I wanted to have it with me in case we ran into that creepy werewolf guy again."

Colette looked at her watch, then looked up at the darkening sky. "Well, it's almost nine. Want to go?"

I stood up. "Yeah," I said. "Let's get this over with."

We walked down the street, wary of the growing shadows around us. Street lights came on, and windows in houses glowed. It was getting dark fast.

When we reached the library, there was only a single light on inside. The building was very quiet. Mrs. Owens' car was the only one in the parking lot.

"Come on," I said, walking a little faster. "It's almost—"

Colette suddenly stopped and grabbed my arm. *"Jeremy!"* she choked, her voice heavy with terror. *"It's . . . it's him! He's right in front of us, hiding in the shadows near the front steps!"*

I didn't see him at first. My eyes darted back and forth like ping pong balls, searching.

Then—

There he was!

He was standing in the shadows, right near the steps. It was almost impossible to see him.

But we knew one thing for certain:

He was waiting for us. He was waiting in darkness, hiding, waiting for us to come along.

Waiting for his chance . . . to turn us into

werewolves!

"Let's try the back door," I whispered. "We'll make a run for it. Ready?"

"Ready," Colette peeped.

"Now!"

We both took off at the same time, wildly running across the grass, around the side of the library, and to the back. There were no lights on behind the building, and it was very, very dark.

"I can't see where I'm going!" Colette said in a strained whisper.

"Neither can I!" I replied. "Just try not to run into anything!"

"How can I try not running into anything when I can't see anything?!?!"

"Never mind," I said. "We have to be close to the back door!"

We ran up to the building, and I began fumbling for a doorknob. I couldn't find anything! No door, or even a window!

"He's coming!" Colette hissed. "I can hear him!"

I looked around and saw the dark shape of a large garbage bin. One of those big ones that they call 'dumpsters'.

It was our only chance.

"*Quick!*" I said, grabbing Colette's arm in the darkness. "*Behind the dumpster! We can hide there!*"

We stumbled forward and ducked behind the large, metal unit. I could hear footsteps now, and I knew that the man was very, very close.

Suddenly, the footsteps slowed. Colette and I remained as quiet as we could.

Jeepers, I thought. *This is the second time today that this has happened!*

We remained huddled behind the dumpster as the footsteps passed us by. When we couldn't hear the man anymore, I stood up. Colette followed.

"*Let's try and sneak back around to the front,*" I said, "*back the way we came. Maybe we can make it before he does.*"

"*Then we can get inside and lock the creep out!*" Colette said.

"*Exactly. Then we'll be safe. But not until we get away from Mr. Freak.*"

We sprinted back around the library, pausing

at the corner to see if the man was anywhere in sight. Not seeing him, we sprang, running like mad in a beeline toward the front steps. I reached them first, with Colette right at my heels.

"We're going to make it!" I said, bounding up the last few steps. *"We're going to make it!"*

I reached the door and pulled . . . but the door didn't budge. I yanked a couple times.

"What's wrong?" Colette shrieked from behind me.

"It's . . . it's locked!" I replied. I glanced through the glass and saw a light on in Mrs. Owens' office. I pounded on the glass.

"Mrs. Owens!" I shouted. *"Mrs. Owens! Open the door!"*

And suddenly . . . *a shadow.* I saw the figure of Mrs. Owens in her office. She was walking toward us!

"There she is!" I cried out in relief.

"Well, I hope she hurries," Colette said. *"Because you-know-who-is coming!"*

I turned to see the dark form of a man running across the library lawn.

"Hurry, Mrs. Owens, Hurry!" I screamed.

And she did. She literally sprang for the door.

By now, the man had reached the steps and he was bounding up them.

"STOP!" he ordered. *"STOP NOW!"*

Yeah, right. Like I was going to listen to a werewolf!

Mrs. Owens reached the door and I stepped aside as she threw it open. *"Inside, children!"* she exclaimed. *"Quickly!"*

I darted through the door . . . but Colette wasn't so lucky. As she tried to go through the door, the man grabbed her shirt.

"No!" she screeched. *"Jeremy! Mrs. Owens! Help me! Help me!!!"*

There was nothing we could do. With a powerful sweep of his arm, the man pulled Colette away. The door slammed closed.

I was safe inside with Mrs. Owens . . . but Colette was gone.

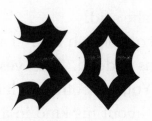

I could see Colette through the glass pane door, struggling and squirming frantically. Suddenly, she broke free from the man's grasp and was at the door! I quickly threw it open and pulled her inside the library.

Outside, the man began to pound at the glass. "No!" he shouted. "You don't understand!"

"Come, children! Into my office! You'll be safe there!"

We hurried through the shadows around

tables and desks, and finally reached Mrs. Owens' office.   Behind us, the man was shouting something from beyond the locked door, but I could no longer understand what he was saying.

"We made it!" Colette said with a heaving gasp. "I thought I was a goner for sure!"

"Well, you're safe now," Mrs. Owens said. "Sit down and rest."

We did as she said.

"He's a werewolf, isn't he?" I asked.

Mrs. Owens nodded. "Yes, yes, a werewolf," she replied. "You are both very lucky."

"I read all about his kind in a book I found today.   Tonight—the first night after a full moon—he was going to turn us into werewolves," I said.

Mrs. Owens nodded. "You know a great deal about werewolves," she said.

"We never thought they were real until today," Colette said.

"Here at the library, we have many books on werewolves," Mrs. Owens said, "but none that talk much about 'real' werewolves. Sit here a moment."

148

Mrs. Owens got up and walked into the dark library.

"There is a lot you can learn here in the library," her voice called out. "I'll show you a few more things that you need to know."

We waited in silence while Mrs. Owens was gone. She was taking a long time, and I kept leaning to the side to see her. Finally, I saw a dark shape emerge from behind a bookshelf—and right away, I knew that we had made a big mistake.

The figure coming toward us *used* to be Mrs. Owens . . . but now, she had changed.

Mrs. Owens was a werewolf!

Suddenly, it all made sense! Mrs. Owens had been the werewolf all along! The man that we thought was so creepy was probably trying to warn us!

I jumped up from the chair and tried to slam the office door closed, but it was too late. Mrs. Owens, the werewolf, was lightning-fast, and she was at the door in a flash. In the light, her features became clear—and she was *gruesome*. Her face, neck and arms were covered with gritty, brown hair. Her mouth was large and long, like a dog's muzzle, and sharp teeth protruded from each side. The sight of her almost made me puke.

Colette screamed as the hideous beast pushed the office door open. The door swung wildly, slamming against the wall.

"You're . . . *you're* . . . the werewolf!" I gasped, backing away from the door.

"You're smart," the werewolf growled, "but you're not quick enough!"

Outside of the library, I heard heavy pounding, then shouting. It was the man that we had thought was the werewolf. He was pounding at the door, trying to get inside.

"It's too late for him to help," the werewolf snarled. "After tonight, you will be a werewolf, just like me!"

I didn't have much time. I quickly forced my hand into my front pocket and pulled out the small vial I had stashed there.

All at once, the werewolf attacked! She leapt across the room, and her feet never touched the ground.

Colette screamed and dove into a corner. I

turned aside and just barely missed one of the werewolves' sharp claws.

I opened up the vial just as the werewolf lunged again.

"Oh, no you don't!" I shouted. In one giant sweep, I emptied the contents of the small bottle. A fine, powdery substance clouded the air, and most of it landed on the attacking werewolf.

The effect was immediate. As soon as the powdery substance touched the creature, a pained, confused look came over its face. It stopped its attack, and seemed to freeze. It was really eerie. The werewolf just stood there like a stone statue.

"What . . . what happened?" Colette stammered. She was still huddled in the corner, her hands doubled into fists and pulled up to her neck.

"I think it worked!" I exclaimed proudly. "That stuff that I made really works!"

All of a sudden, the werewolf began to change. The hair on its face was being pulled back into the skin. The hair on its arms was doing the same thing. And perhaps the strangest of all—its face began to shrink! Its muzzle began to change shape.

The werewolf was changing back into its human form!

It was the weirdest thing I had seen in my entire life. In only a few seconds, a vicious, bloodthirsty creature had become a human . . . *in the form of Mrs. Owens!*

Suddenly, she came to life. She had a confused expression on her face, like she had just awoke and wasn't sure where she was. Then, she smiled and spoke.

"Oh yes. The books about werewolves. That's what you're here for, isn't it?"

Colette and I exchanged puzzled looks.

"And what are you doing in the corner, dear?" Mrs. Owens asked.

"Um . . . I . . . I . . . I dropped my pencil," Colette replied. She stood up.

"Well, never mind that. I have lots of pencils. Here. Here are a few more books about werewolves. I hope that you find what you're looking for in these." She handed several books to me.

"Thank you," I said. "I'm sure they'll be a big

help."

"Well, I don't want to boot you children out, but the library is closed, and I need to get home to Mr. Owens. You children have a good night. And watch out for those werewolves." She winked.

Colette and I laughed nervously. "We will," I said. "We will."

That said, Mrs. Owens led us to the front door. She opened it up and ushered us outside.

"Good night," Mrs. Owens called out.

"Good night!" Colette and I answered, and we hurried down the steps and onto the sidewalk.

Our night of excitement was over.

Or, so we *thought* . . . .

We were hurrying along the sidewalk when a car suddenly came flying through the library parking lot. When the driver saw Colette and me, he slammed on his brakes. I was certain that it was the man that had chased us around the library.

He leapt out of his car. Colette and I stopped, not sure what to do. On one hand, I wanted to run. But, then again, maybe there was more to this story than we knew.

"Are you all right?" the man called out. He began walking toward us.

"Don't come any closer," I said. He stopped and raised his hands.

"I'm not here to hurt you. I only wanted to warn you about your librarian. How did you escape? Where is she?"

"How about *you* tell us about yourself first," Colette answered. "We don't know anything about you."

"I haven't had the time to explain," he said. "My job is not an easy one. But I must know . . . where is Mrs. Owens? There are many people who are in great danger. She is a werewolf, as I am certain you are now aware."

"Not anymore," I said. "I broke the spell."

"What?!?!" the man exclaimed. *"How did you —"*

"You dropped a book by accident when you were chasing us," I said. "I took it home and read it, and found out about all different kinds of werewolves — and how to stop them." I pulled the book from my pocket and handed it back to him. I didn't need it anymore, and besides . . . it didn't belong to me.

"So that's where it went," the man said.

"Thank you for returning it to me."

"Just who *are* you?" I asked him again. "You're not a librarian, are you?"

He chuckled. "Hardly. I am a werewolf hunter. It is my job to seek out werewolves and break their spells."

"You mean . . . it's like a job that you get paid for?" Colette asked.

"Yes," the man said. He continued walking toward us and stopped when he was only a few feet away. Then he reached into his pocket and withdrew a card. He held it out. "Go ahead. Take it."

I took the card from him and held it up to the streetlight. "Nikolas Von Dugan, Professional Werewolf Hunter." Beneath his name an address was listed.

"You're from Germany?!?!" Colette exclaimed, reading the card.

"Well, yes and no, the man said. I'm originally from Germany, but now I live in La Crosse, right here in Wisconsin. Our headquarters—the people I work for—are in Germany."

I nodded. My grandparents live in La Crosse.

"So, you go all over the world?" I asked.

"That is correct. I go wherever I am needed. This year, we've had reports of dozens of werewolves right here in Madison. That's why I'm here—to stop them."

"You . . . You mean there are *more* werewolves around?" Colette asked.

The man nodded. "Even tonight, there are werewolves like Mrs. Owens. Most of them remain in the shadows and in the forests . . . but that doesn't mean that they aren't dangerous. You must be very careful. Especially now that it is dark."

"What about Mrs. Owens?" I asked. "Will she ever remember what's happened to her? Did she even know she was a werewolf?"

"Mrs. Owens, like most werewolves, aren't aware of what they become," Mr. Von Dugan replied.

"You mean . . . she doesn't even know that she turns into a werewolf?" Colette asked.

Mr. Von Dugan shook his head. "Nope. She won't have any memory of becoming a werewolf, or what happened to her tonight.

"But I want you both to remember that there are *still* werewolves around. You *must* be careful."

I looked around, peering into the shadows. It was freaky to think that there might be weird creatures laying in wait for us.

And in fact, we would have one more werewolf encounter . . . and it would happen on our way home . . . *on our very own block!*

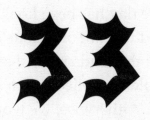

Here's how our final encounter with a werewolf happened.

We said good-by to Mr. Von Dugan. Again, he urged us to be careful, to be watchful. He said he was going to keep hunting until all of the werewolves had been taken care of.

"What a wild day!" Colette remarked as we walked home. The streetlights were on, so we were walking in bright light. Mr. Von Dugan told us that *real* werewolves don't like the light, and they stay in the shadows whenever they can.

"So, Mrs. Owens was a werewolf all along?" Colette asked.

"Yep," I said. "She's been one for a long time. However, she didn't even know it herself. Most people that are werewolves don't even know it themselves."

"That's kooky," Colette said.

"This entire day has been kooky," I agreed.

We stopped in front of Colette's house.

"All is well that ends well," I said.

"Yeah," Colette replied. "I'm sure glad you read that book. Otherwise, we would have been goners."

"I'll call you tomorrow," I said. "We've got to get together and tell everyone what happened. They're going to *freak!*"

I waited while Colette walked toward her house. I don't know . . . I guess I just wanted to make sure she got into her house okay. I really like Colette, and I sure wouldn't want anything to happen to her.

When she reached her porch she waved, opened up the front door, and disappeared inside.

Whew, I thought. *The day is finally over. The*

nightmare has ended.

Nope.

I was only a block from my house. I started walking, feeling pretty proud, since I had single-handedly taken care of a werewolf, all by myself.

Suddenly, I heard a noise in the bushes. It was the sound of snapping twigs.

I stopped. My heart thrashed.

And suddenly, there he was—a werewolf, as big as me . . . lunging from the shadows!

I had no time to move. The hideous creature jumped into the air . . . *and landed right on top of me!*

34

I tried to scream, but my mouth was covered by a large, hairy paw. I fell to the ground in a heap, and the werewolf came down upon me.

The words of Mr. Von Dugan came back to me. *They're still out there, waiting,* he had said. He had told me to be careful.

I hadn't been careful enough.

The werewolf had me pinned to the ground. He started snarling and growling, and I tried to get out from beneath him.

All of a sudden I looked up to see a pair of

sharp fangs.

The werewolf was going to bite me!

I screamed. With all of the strength I could muster, I swung my right arm up and socked the werewolf in the side of the head.

The horrible monster fell sideways. *"Ouch!"* he screeched. *"That hurt! Knock it off!"*

Wait a minute, I thought. *I know that voice!*

I pushed the werewolf off of me and rolled away. Then I stood up, ready for another attack. The werewolf stumbled to his feet, weaving back and forth. He teetered to the left and to the right, and I thought he was going to fall over.

"Owww!" he said. *"That really hurt!"*

And in the next instant, I knew who's voice it was.

Tyler!

I walked up to him and grabbed his face . . . which, of course, wasn't his *real* face . . . it was a *mask!* I yanked hard and it came off. Tyler looked at me dryly, like he was mad.

"That really, *really*, hurt!" he exclaimed, rubbing the side of his head.

"You deserved it, you numbskull," I shot

168

back. "You scared the daylights out of me!"

"I was only kidding," Tyler said. "I found this mask and these fake arms over in the woods. I think they belong to those other kids."

"Well, I'm sorry I hit you," I said, "but I really thought that you were a werewolf."

After we settled down, I told Tyler about my strange day. All he could do was shake his head.

"I *knew* that something freaky was going on!" he exclaimed. "I *knew* it!"

"Well, now we know the truth," I said. "Werewolves really exist!"

But my day wasn't quite over yet . . . for there was one more shocking surprise waiting for me.

35

I had just said good-bye to Tyler and was on my way home.

Suddenly, I saw a dark figure emerge from the shadows down the street. I couldn't tell who it was, but it appeared to be a man.

As I watched, the man suddenly began to change! In less than ten seconds, his body had changed its shape and form . . . and the man had morphed into a werewolf! I could see the strange, pointed ears and the large, hairy arms.

I watched, horrified, as the strange beast

walked. It loped along on its hind legs like a deranged dog. Suddenly, the hideous creature slipped into the shadows.

I'd had just about enough of werewolves, and there was no way I was going to investigate further. I just hoped that Mr. Von Dugan did a good job. I ran home and climbed into bed. It had been a long day.

The next morning, I awoke and called Colette. Then I called a few other friends and we met near the end of the street to play kick ball. I told everyone about the strange things that had happened. No one would have believed me, except Colette was there to back me up.

"It's all true," she said. "Every word of it."

Later that day, I went fishing. I carried my fishing pole and my tackle box down to a creek not far from where we live. There's a place that no one knows about, and the fishing is great.

Well, when I got there, I saw someone sitting on the bank!

How can this be? I wondered, as I got closer.

No one knows about this place!

When I drew near, I could see that it was a girl.

"Hi," I said. She hadn't seen me and she jumped. "Sorry about that," I apologized. "I didn't mean to scare you."

"Oh, you didn't scare me," she replied. "I just didn't know you were there. Besides . . . not much is going to scare me these days."

I was glad to see she wasn't fishing. She was just sitting on the bank of the creek, watching the water go by.

But what did she mean when she said that not much was going to scare her these days?

I was really curious, so I asked her about it.

"Well," she began, "do you know what a mannequin is?"

"A mannequin?" I replied. "Sure. A mannequin is one of those fake plastic people that stores use to display clothes and stuff. A dummy."

She nodded. "That's right," she said. "Well, how would you like it if they came to life?"

"What?!?!" I exclaimed. "No way!"

173

She nodded. "I'll tell you about it if you promise not to laugh."

"Promise," I said, sitting down on the bank next to her.

She began her story, and I forgot all about fishing. I forgot about werewolves. What she told me was freakier than I could have ever imagined . . . .

Next in the
'AMERICAN CHILLERS'® series
by Johnathan Rand:

8:
MINNESOTA
MALL
MANNEQUINS

Turn the page to read a few skin-crawling chapters!

Sometimes when I think about it, I can't believe what happened. It seems like it never happened, like it was all a horrible nightmare.

Or, at the very least, an *awful* dream.

My name is Jessica Harrison, and I live in Bloomington, Minnesota. Minnesota is in the northern midwestern part of the United States. It's in a part of the country where we have lots of lakes, and four very different seasons: spring, summer, fall, and winter. Bloomington is a pretty cool place to live. The best part about it is that it's in the same city as the hugest mall on the planet, The Mall of America. In case you've never heard of it, this mall is so big that there is even an amusement park in it, and not one of those dinky ones with only a couple rides. *This one is 7 acres big!* There are also over 500 stores and restaurants.

Pretty incredible, I know.

But what happened to me in this mall is even *more incredible* than that.

My mom and dad have always been pretty cool about me going places as long as there is a chaperone. You know — someone older to watch over you. I do have an older brother named Mark, and I always beg him to take me to the mall. But he just got his drivers license, so he goes there with all his cool friends. I just wish my brother and his friends would've been at the mall on the most terrifying night of my life!

It all started when one of my teachers, Mrs. Shoquist, planned a field trip to the Mall. School had just started and this was the first trip of the year. In one of my new classes, we're learning how to run a store. Our whole class was really excited, especially me and my best friend, Rachel Owens. We love clothes, and we decided that someday, we would have our own clothing store . . . maybe even our *own* line of clothes.

Rachel is one of the most popular girls in school, but she isn't a snob or anything. She just loves clothes as much as I do. Her favorite outfit is jeans with really fancy shirts.

That's one of the reasons that we love to go to the mall, to look at the clothes. We couldn't wait for this field trip . . . especially since Rachel and I had a secret.

We had decided that when we got to the mall we would sneak off to see the new clothes. If we snuck away, we could cover all of the stores and be back just in time to catch the bus back to school. Mrs. Shoquist wouldn't even miss us. She was really nice, but sometimes she acted a little — well — *odd*. Not many people knew this, though. This was our secret . . . and it was a secret that would lead to the most shocking, horrible experience of our whole lives.

2

The bus for the field trip pulled up to the mall at noon. We all had to wear school nametags, just in case we got separated from the group . . . which is exactly what Rachel and I wanted to do. We thought that we knew our way around this mall, even though it is so gigantic. It's so huge that people come to the Mall of America on their vacation—that's just how fun it is. But it wasn't going to be fun today, not for Rachel and I anyway.

When we got inside the mall, the first thing we got to do was have lunch in the food court. Yum! There are lots of great places to eat, and lots of different restaurants to choose from. And, it was always so busy there that we thought this would be the perfect place to sneak away.

We each got to pick the place where we would eat. I decided to have Chinese food and Rachel went for pizza. We ate quickly, then just acted like we were taking our trays back. We were about to make a clean getaway to go explore . . . but the biggest blabbermouth of the whole class—Riley Kline—yelled out that we were leaving without permission. We stopped dead in our tracks. With quick thinking we ducked down into two other chairs and acted like we were still eating.

We thought for sure that big mouth Riley had jinxed our plan. When Mrs. Shoquist looked at us, we smiled and shrugged our shoulders like we didn't know what Riley was talking about. Mrs. Shoquist nodded at us and gave Riley a scolding look. Then, when she turned her head we stuck our tongues out at Riley. This made Riley so mad that she finally just looked away.

When the coast was clear, we slowly got up again and snuck to the tray return. When we got there we looked around, just to make sure that nobody saw us.

"*Anybody watching?*" I whispered to Rachel.

"*Nope,*" she replied. "*I don't see anyone.*"

We stood there for a minute, then we made a run for it to the other side of a big fountain and ducked behind it. We took off our nametags and stuck them in our backpacks, so that nobody would know we weren't where we belonged.

We were in the clear! Operation "Sneak-Away" was a success . . . or so we *thought.*

Little did we know that somebody was looking. From the moment we got off the bus, we were all being watched.

Not only were we being watched . . . but as we walked towards our favorite store, we were being *followed!*

No sooner had we gotten right in front of the store than a large, freaky-looking hand reached out to stop us.

I gasped.

Rachel gasped.

We both jumped. We were in trouble now, but it was just the beginning of our nightmare.

3

A man was glaring down at us, and when we saw his face, Rachel and I gasped again.

Something about this man was *really* creepy. He had frozen black eyes, and a nasty snarl on his face. He seemed to be taller than anyone I ever knew, and he had slicked-back black hair that almost looked plastic.

"What do you think your doing?" he said, in a tone that would make your skin crawl.

"I . . . I . . . we . . . we . . ." Rachel stuttered. She was so scared she couldn't even speak.

"We're with a class field trip, sir", I said. I fumbled for my nametag in my backpack to show him, but I was so nervous I couldn't find it.

"Then why aren't you with your field trip?" he sneered.

"We are! Really!" I said.

"I don't believe you!" he shot back. "You're coming with me!" Then he made us walk in front of him. We just looked at each other. Now Rachel was more mad than afraid. But this man had on a blue uniform, a walkie-talkie, and even a badge. Our mothers would be so mad at us. Mrs. Shoquist, too. I was sure that it would be a long time before we got to the mall again, if ever.

But what we didn't know was that it would be a long, long time before we even got out of the mall.

It seemed like we were walking forever when I realized that he wasn't taking us back to the group at all. We headed down a long, dark hallway. When I asked him where we were going, he just glared at me with a blank, strange look on his face.

"Rachel," I whispered quietly without turning my head. *"He . . . doesn't look real!"*

"No," Rachel replied. *"He doesn't. He looks like a robot or something."*

We turned the corner to another scary, empty hallway. I had never been in this part of the mall before and I don't think that Rachel had, either. He unlocked a door.

"Wait in here," he ordered us in that creepy voice of his.

Afraid to make him mad, we did what he said.

He slammed the door behind us. Wherever we were, it was *cold* . . . and so dark that I couldn't see my hand in front of my face. We stood there, petrified with fear, too scared to move. Then we could hear the lock turn, and his loud footsteps walking away. I knew we were in a lot of trouble already . . . but things were about to get worse.

4

The first thing I did after I heard his footsteps fade away was to try and find a light switch. I would be a lot less frightened if I could see where we were at!

I groped in the dark until I felt something cold and metal.

The doorknob! The light switch has to be here somewhere!

I placed the palms of my hands on the wall and swept them around. After a moment, my left hand touched a small nub on the wall.

Please, I thought, *please be a light switch.*

I flipped it on and bright light flooded all around . . .and Rachel and I couldn't believe our eyes.

We were in a tiny, box-like room. No windows, no doors, nothing.

"Jessica, what's going on?" asked Rachel.

"I don't know," I replied, shaking my head. "Maybe he thinks we stole something." Which seemed just silly to me because I would never steal anything in my life. Neither would Rachel.

Then I started thinking about that strange man again.

"You know," I began, "there was something very odd about that guy. He almost looked fake, like he wasn't human. Like one of those store mannequins."

"A *what?*" asked Rachel.

"You know . . . those fake models that they put the clothes on. They look like plastic humans."

"Oh yeah," said Rachel. "Mannequins. I think that was something that we were going to learn about today."

It seemed like we were locked in that room

forever.

Finally, we heard noises.   Rachel and I listened as we stared at the door in terror. In a way, we were glad someone was coming for us, because we had been alone for so long.

But I knew that something was not right . . . and that's what scared both of us.

Now we could hear footsteps coming down the hall . . . the same shuffling sounds that the guard made when he walked.   But as the footsteps drew nearer, it sounded like there was more than just one person.

Then we could hear talking. I could hear a woman's voice.

"Rachel!" I whispered. *"That sounds like Mrs. Luchien, the mall manager!"* She was the woman that had come to our class to talk about the mall with us kids. Maybe everything would be ok now that she was here.

Boy, was I wrong.

They were getting closer. Their voices got clearer as I could hear that freaky-looking security guard saying that he had told our teacher that we were in the room and we couldn't get out.

"Splendid," Mrs. Luchien said. "We can't have any nosy kids foiling our plans."

Rachel and I freaked. All along, we had *thought* that something was wrong.

Now, we *knew* it.

And we knew something else: we had to get out of there. We had to escape somehow.

I ran over to a big metal vent in the corner of the room and tried to pry it off, but it was no use. I started digging frantically in my backpack.

"What are you looking for?" asked Rachel.

"Something to pry that vent off with," I replied. "We have *got* to get out of here."

Rachel started to dig in her backpack, too.

"I've got it!" she exclaimed, pulling out her nametag and ran over to the vent. The thick plastic of the tag was just the right size to wedge the vent from the wall just enough so that we could pull it off.

On the other side of the door, I could hear keys jingling.

"Hurry!" I hissed. *"They're almost here!"*

Rachel snapped the vent cover off just as I could hear keys being pushed into the lock. I grabbed my backpack, ran over and followed her through the vent.

There was another room on the other side of the one we were in!

Thinking quickly, I reached through the vent hole, grabbed the cover, and pulled it back on, just as we heard the door open.

Whew! That had been a close one . . . but where were we *now?* The room we were in was like some huge storage room with lots of boxes and crates.

"Where are we?" Rachel wondered aloud, her voice just barely a whisper.

"I don't know," I replied quietly. *"But look! There's a window over there!"*

We tip-toed to the window . . . but when we saw what was on the other side of the glass, we both gasped at the same time.

"Oh no!" I said.

Below us was the parking lot . . . *but it was empty!* It was night, and there wasn't a single car to be seen anywhere.

Just then, in the other room, we heard shouting. It was Mrs. Luchien . . . and she wasn't happy that we'd escaped.

"Find them!" she shouted. "I don't care what it takes! We *must* find them!"

"*Jessica?*" Rachel peeped.

"*Yeah?*" I replied.

"*I think we're in a lot of trouble.*"

I would have answered, but I didn't need to. I *knew* we were in for it.

And when a door suddenly sprang open, I knew that the real trouble had started.

5

"We have got to find them now!" I heard Mrs. Luchien scream. "We *must* find them!"

Wow, I thought. *What did we do to make her so mad at us?*

Rachel and I ducked down behind some boxes. We didn't make a sound until we heard the door slam. Then we heard the footsteps and voices moving away.

From where we were hidden we could see another window, but on the other side of the glass was another room. A faint glow illuminated boxes that were stamped "WIGS". There were *hundreds* of boxes of wigs. I thought that was odd.

"I'll bet that's where the security guard got his

hair," I whispered. Rachel giggled.

We waited for a moment, hunched down behind the boxes. We wanted to make sure those two creepy people were gone.

"I think the coast is clear," said Rachel.

We tiptoed to the door. Luckily, it wasn't locked. We hurried down the hallway as quietly as we could, on the lookout for Mrs. Luchien and the weirdo security guard dude.

We passed lots of hallways and corridors.

"Gosh, Jess," Rachel said quietly. *"I hope we don't get lost."*

Finally, we could see the light from the main mall area ahead. We knew that we had to be really careful, just in case they were waiting for us at the end of the hall.

When we got to the end of the hallway we slowly peered around the corner. The mall was completely empty.

"Something is really strange," said Rachel.

"Yeah," I agreed. "There should be night crews around, cleaning things up and stuff."

Then we noticed that we were right next to Macy's, which is a *huge* department store. The main entrance door was wide open. I thought that was weird. Weren't they supposed to lock up all the stores at night?

"I bet that we can get outside through Macy's", I said.

Rachel's eyes lit up. "I *know* that we can! My sister used to work there, and they always left the emergency exits open from the inside. Follow me!"

We ducked down and ran as fast as we could into the open doors and behind the racks of clothes. We needed to hurry, but we also wanted to make sure that no one saw us.

Just then, Rachel stopped, and I bumped into her.

"What's wrong?" I asked. *"Rachel? Rachel?"*

"Did you see that?" she said.

"See what?" I replied.

Just then, Rachel ducked into a rack of clothing. She was completely hidden.

"Jess! Hide!"

I slipped into the same rack, and now I was right beside her. We were both hidden within dozens of hanging garments.

Rachel reached out and made an opening in the clothing so we could see around the mall—and it was then that I saw what had scared Rachel.

Mannequins . . . the plastic figures that were used to display clothing . . . were coming to life all around the store!

ABOUT THE AUTHOR

Johnathan Rand is the author of more than 65 books, with we
over 4 million copies in print. Series include **AMERICAN**
CHILLERS, MICHIGAN CHILLERS, FREDDI
FERNORTNER, FEARLESS FIRST GRADER, and **TH**
ADVENTURE CLUB. He's also co-authored a novel for teer
(with Christopher Knight) entitled **PANDEMIA**. When not trav
eling, Rand lives in northern Michigan with his wife and thre
dogs. He is also the only author in the world to have a store tha
sells only his works: **CHILLERMANIA!** is located in India
River, Michigan. Johnathan Rand is not always at the store, but h
has been known to drop by frequently. Find out more at:

www.americanchillers.com

Also by Johnathan Rand:

GHOST IN THE GRAVEYARD

FUN FACTS ABOUT WISCONSIN:

State Capitol: Madison

State Rock: Red Granite

State Wildlife Animal: White-Tailed Deer

State Bird: Robin

State Animal: Badger

State Tree: Sugar Maple

State Fish: Muskellunge

State Flower: Wood Violet

State Insect: Honeybee

State Fossil: Trilobite

FAMOUS PEOPLE FROM WISCONSIN!

Woody Herman, band leader

Laura Ingalls Wilder, author

Harry Houdini, magician

Orson Welles, actor and producer

Frank Lloyd Wright, architecht

among many others!

Join the official

AMERICAN CHILLERS

FAN CLUB!

Visit www.americanchillers.com for details

Johnathan Rand travels internationally for school visits and book signings! For booking information, call:

1 (231) 238-0338!

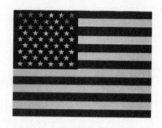

USA